Bone Song

SHERRYL CLARK

Ransom

Bone Song

SHERRYL CLARK

Series Editor: Peter Lancett

Published by Ransom Publishing Ltd.
51 Southgate Street, Winchester, Hampshire SO23 9EH, UK
www.ransom.co.uk

ISBN 978 184167 751 4

First published in 2009
Copyright © 2009 Ransom Publishing Ltd.
Cover by Flame Design, Cape Town, South Africa
Front cover photograph: Lucia Constantin

Award-winning author Sherryl Clark lives in Victoria, Australia where she teaches professional writing and editing at Victoria University. She writes for children, young adults and adults and has had more than thirty books published. When not teaching she visits schools and runs workshops and seminars on writing and editing.

IN THE SAME SERIES

CHAPTER 1
Melissa

Probably my whole class is laughing at me right now. Goody-goody Melissa McCardle in detention for three whole days after school. I bet they're dying to find out what I did to get here too, but I'm not telling.

This room is the pits. And it stinks. I mean, it really stinks. It's like two basketball teams have left all their sweaty runners in here to go mouldy, then thrown in a few banana peels and apple cores for good measure. There's one tiny window high up, and the room only fits a dozen desks.

God, I'm sitting in the front row again. Why do I do that? I thought I'd cured myself of the habit. Footsteps echo along the corridor. Two sets. There's just enough time to throw myself towards the back of the room, school bag first, and reach for a chair. I miss. Of course. When the door opens, I'm lying flat on my face on the floor.

'Miss McCardle, I presume?'

I recognise the voice straight away. It's Mr Feibler, the PE teacher. As I hurry to get up, banging my elbow on a desk so hard I think my arm is going to fall off, all I see is his tanned, hairy legs and his tight, white shorts.

'Yeah, that's me,' I mumble.

'Here's your cellmate. Deborah Lessing.'

'Dobie!' the girl behind him hisses.

Oh no, it's her. Right away, I feel the water from the hose splattering me all over again, my threadbare T-shirt sticking to me, the boys laughing... The red haze rises up in front of my eyes. I take a few deep breaths, trying to will it back down again. It's got me into trouble once already at this school. I can't afford to let it take over again. But I remember what Dobie did to me. I can't stand the sight of her. This is going to be the longest detention in history.

I keep my eyes focused on Mr Feibler's snow-white Nikes, because that's safer, and listen as he runs through the rules.

'I hope you've both brought homework to do, or at least a book to read.' A snort from Dobie. 'No talking, no leaving the room. Do either of you want to go to the toilet? Because I've got a basketball team to coach. I can't be running backwards and forwards all afternoon. No? Right. I'll check on you every half hour or so.'

He slams the door behind him and his footsteps speed up. He obviously can't wait to get away from us.

'Every half hour. Yeah, right. We'll be lucky if he comes back at all!'

Well, she would know, wouldn't she? Miss Deborah Lessing, who insists everyone call her Dobie and ignores the ones who call her No-brain. She spends nearly half her afternoons here in this room. I should've remembered that before I went berserk. It's a double punishment, being here with her.

I sit down at the desk in the furthest corner and get out my maths homework. Count this as a blessing, I tell myself, a chance to actually get my homework done properly, in peace. Sometimes it's nearly midnight before I get Mum settled in bed asleep. Homework, by then, gets done in a mad rush.

'You're not actually going to do work, are you?'

She's sitting on the desk by the door, shaking a bottle of dark purple nail polish. I shrug. It's none of her business. 'Don't talk to me.' It snaps out of my mouth before I can stop it.

'Oohh. Afraid I'll corrupt you, sweetie pie? Too late, you're already in here. In the dungeon with Big Bad Dobie. All hope is gone!' She sneers, making the rings and studs dotted around her face wiggle. When she sticks out her tongue at me, I see the stud through it and my skin crawls.

'Just shut up and leave me alone.' I turn my back on her so I don't have to look at her ugly, studded face. She is such a weirdo, and she plays on it. She likes to put her heavy boots up on her desk to drive the teachers crazy. She's been caught smoking heaps of times.

Everyone said she graffitied the wall behind the teachers' car park with the words 'School sucks, and teachers suck...' Half the kids were busting to add their own list of what comes next, but the principal found it in time and got it cleaned off. What Dobie doesn't know is that *I know she didn't do it*. I saw some tenth graders spraying the wall, but she still took the blame. I wondered why, but it served her right. She had to pay for the cleaning, or her parents did. From what I hear, they're revoltingly rich and she gets heaps of pocket money. I hope they made *her* pay for it.

I focus on my algebra, trying to ignore the sharp smell of nail polish. Why am I wasting time thinking about a loser like her? I've got more important things on my mind. Like how I'm going to get home before Mum. Or if I don't, what am I going to tell her? She'll freak out if I tell her I got detention. *Don't call attention to yourself.* She must've said it a million times.

The algebra problem blurs on the page. I blink hard. What time is it? Have I only been here for fifteen minutes? Maybe I'll try English instead. Ms Rogers has been reading *Wuthering Heights* to us in class. She must think most of the kids are too dumb to read it on their own. She's probably right. Now we have to write a poem inspired by the story. I hate this kind of thing. I like to write my poems for myself, not for any stupid teacher to criticise. I close my eyes and force myself to imagine the moors, the wind and the dark trees.

'Hey, you're not writing that for Roger Ramjet's class, are you?' Dobie leans over me and I smell sour cigarettes on her clothes.

'What if I am?' I curl my arm around my notebook.

'You could write one for me. I might even pay you.'

'Get stuffed. Why can't you write your own?'

'Nah, poetry's not my thing. I like songs better.'

'So write a song! Just leave me alone.'

She strolls back to the desk by the door, humming, and dumps her bag down, rummaging through it. I peek over my shoulder, even though I couldn't care less what she's doing. She's flicking through a scruffy notebook, a purple pen in her mouth. She keeps humming the same stupid tune over and over, scribbling every now and then.

She's put me off writing poems now. I'd rather stab her with my pen to get some silence for a change. I go back to algebra, trying to focus on solving the gigantic problem in front of me but it seems like a big mish-mash of letters and numbers that just won't make sense. Once upon a time, I used to be a superstar at maths.

It's her fault I can't concentrate. How am I going to stand being here with her for three whole afternoons? If I'm lucky, this'll be her last day. I ask, 'How long are you in detention for?'

'Huh? Oh, a week this time, I think. I don't know, I lose track.' When she sees my face fall, she says, 'If you can't do the time, don't do the crime.'

'Why are you here so often? Why can't you just...'

'Behave? Conform? Be a little goody like you?'

'I'm not a goody. I... I have to...'

'Be Mummy's little girl?'

'No! Anyway, what's wrong with getting on OK with your mother?' For me though it's more like mummy-sitting half the time.

She laughs, but it sounds like she's choking. 'Hey, that's why I'm always here. So I don't *have* to go home to my mother.' Her face darkens, she looks away. 'Forget I said that. Go back to your homework, *Goody.*'

Before I can respond, she opens the door and leaves.

I hope Mr Feibler comes back, finds her gone and gives her more detention. It'd serve her right. But somehow I think she wouldn't care at all. Whatever. Not my problem.

My problem might be to get through these three afternoons without killing her.

CHAPTER 2
Dobie

Of all the people who had to get detention this week, why did it have to be smarmy Melissa McCardle? That's my space, even if it is smelly and small. I've got pacing down to a fine art, ten steps up, ten steps back. It drives my mother crazy, especially when I do it in the hallway in my big black boots while she's backstabbing someone on the phone.

Mind you, there's one kind of gossip Mother hates. The stuff about me, my latest *shenanigans*, as she calls them, in an effort to make them sound trivial. I try to time it so that I manage to get into trouble again just when she's relaxing, thinking that I'm going to behave for a while.

I pace the dark echoing corridor outside the dungeon, ten steps each way, but it's not as much fun when there's no one to annoy. Goody McCardle probably hopes I'll skip out, that *Feeble* will come back and I'll be in even bigger trouble. To tell the truth, I can't be bothered. It's only Thursday but I feel like the week has been about ten days long already. I'm so tired.

That tune is still in my head; little bits keep adding themselves. I have to write more of it down but I'm not going back in there with Goody. She's always so well behaved, it makes me sick. Her and my mother would love each other. She wasn't happy when she saw me arrive. Why was she on the floor? What a loser.

I slide down to the tiled floor and pull out my notebook again. I've almost got the refrain right. And one line *Bring a bell and ring it just for me.* But the next line won't come so I stop trying to force it, just let the melody run. Goody would probably say I should write more poetry then the song lyrics would develop more easily. What would she know?

People like her really bug me. She always sits quietly, passes tests, does her homework – like it matters. What does she think this stupid school is going to teach her? At least they had music and art at that pathetic private school my mother sent me to. Here they don't even have enough money to buy decent computers. Mother Dear would say I brought it on myself. But being expelled is no big deal. Not really.

I hear footsteps but I don't move. It sounds like *Feeble*, and it is. He bounces along in those tight shorts and Nikes like they came with a free bottle of Viagra. A bit sickening on someone as old as him; he's at least thirty.

'Aren't you supposed to be inside the detention room, Ms Lessing?'

Gee, so witty. He should know that sarcasm is lost on me. 'I think I was disturbing Ms McCardle.' He arches his eyebrows like he's expecting something more.

'I believe I was breathing her air.'

'You know the rules. Back inside, hurry up.'

'Jeez.' I get up and he opens the door for me, waits until I step inside and then slams it behind me.

Goody turns her back on me, which suits me fine. I sit down at the desk by the door again and try to hum my way back into my new song but it won't work. The main thread of it has gone. Just as well I wrote down all the notes. When I get home, I'll lock my bedroom door and get my guitar out. With a bit of luck, Mother won't even notice I'm there if I don't go down for dinner. Nancy always hides a pile of leftovers for me in the back of the fridge. Now that's pathetic – the only person who cares about me is the housekeeper.

I'm bored. Usually I wander around the school and amuse myself. The things I've overheard by hanging around outside the staffroom are pretty amazing. I know everything that goes on in this school; who's got problems at home, who's in trouble...

Why *is* Goody McCardle in detention? She's usually too busy licking the teacher's shoes clean to make trouble. Suddenly the question is burning a hole in my brain.

'Hey, Goody, what did you accomplish to end up in this luxury accommodation?'

'Huh?' She gazes at me with bleary eyes.

I try again. 'How come you're in the hole with me? You kill someone?' I bare my teeth at her but she's not fooled that it's a smile.

'None of your business.'

'If you didn't kill anyone, maybe you... slept with the principal and Mrs Gregson found out? She's sleeping with him too, you know.'

'Don't be so stupid.'

'Don't stop there, throw me some real compliments. How about dork-brain or pea-brain, or maybe...' I screw my face up, pretend I'm thinking hard, 'No-brain.'

She turns bright red and I know she's heard the other kids call me that. No big deal. I'll get them all back one day. Maybe I'll post all their private miseries on the notice boards around the school. I bet everyone would like to know that Robbie Wilson still wets the bed, Mandy Foster left school last week because she's pregnant and Jason Benbow's mother is an alcoholic.

Goody's turned her back on me again and, for some strange reason, that irritates the hell out of me. 'If you tell me why you're here, I promise I won't tell a soul. It'll be our little secret.' All that gets me is her middle finger jerking over her shoulder. 'I'll tell you why I'm here first then.'

'Why? I don't care. It'll be for some dumb reason, like that boring graffiti.'

I sniff and shake my head. Why *had* I taken the blame for that one? It hadn't even been clever.

'Actually, that wasn't me, thank you very much. If I was going to paint words on the wall, they'd be a lot more original than that infantile attempt.'

'I know,' she said.

What does she know? I change the subject to stir her up. 'Have you written a poem for me yet? Can I see your notebook?'

I walk across the room and lean over her.

'Go away!' She huddles over her notebook. For the first time I hear something in her voice – is it panic? Shall I push her harder or back off? I can't decide.

The door opens. It's *Feeble*.

'Pack up your stuff, girls, you've got a reprieve for today. I've got to take Jamie to the hospital – broken wrist, I think.'

Before I can open my mouth to say anything, he's gone, running down the corridor. Shit. I've got no money to eat at the shopping centre. I'll have to go home. I feel sick.

CHAPTER 3
Melissa

Great! If I hurry, I might just make it home before Mum. I won't have time to shop but there must be something in the cupboards I can cook.

I throw my books into my bag and head for the door. Dobie is fiddling with her bag, hanging back.

'Can't stand to leave?' I ask. She doesn't answer and I push past her. I don't want to think about tomorrow, how I'll have to be in here with her again. I hurry down the corridor to the exit door, run to the school gate and down the street, my bag thumping on my back. The three blocks to our place seem like three miles.

I don't bother with the elevator – it'll be full of pee and empty beer bottles. Up the stairs. By the fourth flight, I can hardly breathe, then I trip and fall. Pain jags through my right knee and elbow. I scream.

'You stupid bitch,' I mutter over and over. It helps to force me up, keep me moving. By the time I get to my front door, snot is dripping from my nose and my hand shakes so much I can't get the key in the lock. I take a deep breath, try again. The flat is empty so I head for the bathroom to wash my face.

Quick, quick, into the kitchen, check the cupboards and the fridge. Bread, margarine, cheese, one small egg. Mum can have that. I'll make her a cheese omelette with toast. I can maybe have a toasted sandwich. The clock is showing 5.30 – she's late.

That pulls me up in a hurry. She's never late, unless... No, she can't be in a bar. It's not payday until tomorrow. No money. I go over the possibilities in my head and I feel sick. She must have found someone to buy her a drink. Some guy who doesn't know she's on tranks and that she'll fall over unconscious after the third glass of wine.

I don't know what to do. I could go to her work – no, I can't. She started a new temp job yesterday and I don't know where it is.

I look down and find I'm wringing my hands like one of those old Italian grandmas in the movies. Maybe she's doing overtime. Yeah, that's it. New job, busy place, lots to catch up. That's gotta be it.

But I know it's not. I've been ignoring the signs. The loopy laugh, the trembling, the sneaking of the extra pill.

I toss the food back in the fridge and grab a jacket. Sometimes she picks a bar close to home. I hope that's what she's done. God, I hope so. If she gets arrested and her name goes into the computer, we'll have to run again.

I'm so tired...

I shrug into my jacket as I head down the stairs. I'm dreading trawling the pubs. This is such a crap neighbourhood, and it'll be dark soon. I stick close to the walls and start with *Jacko's Place*, a real dive. I've had lots of practice at this – I slip in through the doorway, scan the crowd and listen for her high-pitched laugh, then I'm outta there.

What was she wearing this morning? Blue striped shirt, I think, and black skirt. Four bars later, no luck. Sweat coats my face and trickles down my back. There's only one more bar in this street; the next one is a couple of blocks away. It's dark in the doorways and corners. Panic grabs at my throat. Two cars glide past, a horn toots. I hunch down and scurry along the street.

The *Caledonia Club* looms in front of me. It's a bit posh for this area, with a threadbare red carpet in front of the brass-handled oak door. I can hear jazz music coming from inside, along with laughter. Two men burst through the door, and a rush of friendly warmth seems to reach out before the door swings back again.

That's when I hear her laugh.

God, I want to kill her! I'm out here looking for her, dodging weirdos in cars, and she's in there drinking and laughing. How could she do that? I want to go in there and drag her out by her hair! The red haze is back, like blood smeared across my eyes, and I half-sob, then take a deep breath.

Cool it. Yelling at her isn't going to help. She might even just refuse to come home. Depends how many drinks she's had already. And who she's with. If she's with her new boss, I'd better not cause trouble.

I take a few more breaths, then I pull the big door open and go in. The *Caledonia Club* is wide but not very deep. I'm facing the bar so I slip sideways around the doorway before the barman can spot me and order me out. The tall potted plant is handy for hiding behind, even if its plastic leaves are coated with dust. A million people have stubbed out their cigarettes in the pot. A quick scan to my right but no Mum, so I scuttle across the doorway to check the other side.

There she is in a booth, leaning back, cheeks flushed, opposite a blond guy in a dark suit. I don't like the way he's looking at her, as if he knows it'll only take one more drink and she'll do whatever he suggests. Does he know about the pills she's on? I do a quick shuffle to the booth, slide in next to her.

'Hi, Mum, I'm ready now.' I say it brightly like this is something we've arranged.

She stares at me for a moment. I hold my breath. Is she going to play along? Then her face relaxes and her eyes grow warm.

'Hi, sweetie.'

She doesn't ask how I found her, so I've caught her at just the right stage.

'If we don't go now, we're going to be late.' I grab her hand, tug gently. She resists and my heart takes a nosedive.

'Melissa, I want you to meet Gordon. He's the sales manager at my new place. He's made me feel very welcome.'

I'll bet he has. 'Hi, Gordon,' I say nicely, then back to her. 'Mum, you promised we'd be on time tonight. This school thing is really important.'

'Oh.' She looks puzzled.

Of course you don't remember any school thing, Mum, there isn't one. For God's sake, get up and come with me without arguing, please. I tug her hand again. This time she starts to move.

'I guess duty calls, Gordon. Sorry.' She smiles at him. 'See you at work tomorrow.'

He looks sour but that's his problem. He can go home to his wife now. I let Mum make her own way to the door – she gets snappy with me if I help her in public. Outside, I take her arm and she cuddles in close to me.

'What's on at school, sweetie?' She's definitely slurring now. There's no money for a taxi and I'm stuffed if I can carry her. I hurry her along a bit more.

'It's a parent thing, and we're late. We'll have to speed up, come on.' Oddly enough, the faster I hassle her along, the straighter she walks. Lucky she's got her sensible work shoes on. I can feel the bones in her hand, like an old hen I'd once picked up on a farm visit in primary school.

'Steady Mum, we're nearly home. Look, the elevator.' I pray that it's working – for once, it is. Of course, it stinks of pee and vomit and there's a pile of paper in one corner that I don't want to look at too closely. I press the button and the doors close.

It's all going OK. Mum hasn't questioned why we're home instead of at school. If I can get her to eat something, we'll be on a roll. She starts to stagger just before we get to our front door and I can't hold her. She drops to her knees as I reach for my key to get her inside as fast as I can, but it's not in my pocket.

How many stupid damn things can you do in one day, you idiot? The tears burn in my eyes but I force them back. Maybe Mrs Wyatt will be home. She keeps a spare key for me, and sometimes lends me money. I roll Mum around awkwardly and manage to lean her against the wall, then knock on Mrs Wyatt's door – but there's no reply. Bingo night. She won't be back until after nine.

Everything comes crunching down on me all at once. I don't know whether to cry or scream, but I haven't got enough energy to do either. My knee is killing me. How come I didn't feel it before? I look down at it, stunned when I see all the dried blood in streams down my leg. The top of my sock is soaked and turning brown.

Mum starts to slide sideways. I haul her straight again, then sit down beside her, letting her fall against me. Her head lolls on my shoulder; I hear her breathing, deep and throaty. If she took another trank before she went to the bar, she'll be out all night now. I really, truly hope Mrs Wyatt's son walks her home tonight, so he can help me carry Mum inside. I close my eyes and try to think of absolutely nothing.

CHAPTER 4
Dobie

I hang around the school for about ten minutes until I realise I'm behaving like a total dork – I mean, who stays at school if they don't have to? I wait at the bus stop, kind of hoping the bus is cancelled but it turns up in a couple of minutes just to spite me. I walk all the way to the back, ignoring the two old ladies in their floral dresses and big white handbags who purse their lips at my studs and hair.

The bus driver is staring at me in his rear-view mirror. Does he think I'm going to start a riot on my own? Hey, that might be something new to torment my mother with.

The bus passes Middle Gate and the street leading down to the Housing Commission flats. All the way down, four-storey cement-sheet buildings create a wall of grey squares and red glass, the sunset reflected in the windows. It looks really cool but I'd hate to live there. It's bad enough going to school with some of the kids from that street.

I wonder what my mother thinks of them. Maybe she's waiting for me to get hooked on drugs so she can ship me off to a *facility* where she doesn't have to see me or think about me. Likewise Sara and Louise. Dad might miss me though. I hope.

Anyway, there's no way I'll get into drugs. Had enough of that in the hospital, feeling like the world was coated in fuzz and everyone was talking in a tunnel. Oops, daydreaming so much that I nearly missed my stop. If I had two dollars, I could buy some chocolate before my next bus arrives, but I know that I'm practically broke. Bummer. Have I still got a chocolate stash behind my books? Or did I actually get up in the middle of the night last night and eat it all? Might have dreamt that.

The second bus takes forever to weave its way through the business district and into my suburb. Tall office buildings followed by houses with marble columns and too many windows. I get off and wander down my street where everyone has a gardener, and I stop to admire neat little hedges and blooming roses. I've been tempted a few times to come along after dark and spray weedkiller on everything, but if the neighbours didn't guess it was me, my mother would and she'd go ballistic. I'd probably be grounded, which would be the ultimate punishment for both of us. She tries to avoid that unless she's so pissed off that she can't help herself.

I stop in front of our house – who's inside? Dad's car isn't here, but Mother's is. Classical music drifts from somewhere upstairs. I guess Louise is home. It's Thursday so maybe Sara is still at choir practice. If Mother isn't in the kitchen bossing Nancy around and driving her nuts, I'll be able to sneak in without being seen.

I follow the side path around to the back door, open it quietly, slip inside and creep up the passageway towards the kitchen. A voice I know only too well pierces the closed door. I'm about to get the hell up to my room when I catch what she's actually saying.

'Of course, it's only to be expected that they'll set new rules for Deborah. She'll just have to make sure she abides by them.'

Nancy murmurs something but Mother talks over the top of her, like she always does. I swear Nancy could tell her the house was on fire and Mother wouldn't hear. But I want to know about these rules.

'Madeline Le Blanc is a very reasonable woman. And a sizable donation to the school library didn't go astray.' Mother laughs – the dry, sarcastic laugh that she saves for discussing topics of money and sex. 'That girl will just have to shape up, or else.'

Or else what? My control-freak mother has obviously bribed Barton Private School for Young Ladies into taking me back. That sure makes them stupider than snot on the sidewalk. I turn the handle and shove open the kitchen door. It bangs against the wall and Mother jumps.

'I am not going back to Barton,' I say, matching her glare.

'You'll do as you're told.'

'I'll just do something to make them expel me again.' There are lots of things I've learned at my new school that would really freak out the Barton Bigots.

Mother walks towards me, stopping two paces away. She doesn't want Nancy to hear, I can tell. 'You will either go back to Barton and behave, or you will be put in a boarding school that specialises in problem children. Somewhere a long way from here.'

I can't believe the venom in her voice. Suddenly I realise she might hate me as much as I hate her. Wow. I can't think what to say. It's like my brain is jammed. She's got that little light of victory in her eyes and she smiles at me, then leaves the kitchen. I'm no longer worth talking to.

Nancy had her head down, chopping spinach, but she looks up at me and grimaces. 'Man, you sure put a stick up her bum. What've you done now?'

'Nothing. Well, nothing new.'

'You in detention again?'

'Yeah. That's normal, isn't it?'

Nancy doesn't answer, thinks for a moment. 'She was ferreting around upstairs this morning for half an hour or more.'

Oh shit. She's been in my room, I just know it. Suddenly my legs come to life. I bolt out of the kitchen and up the stairs, all the time trying to remember what things I've stashed and where. Chocolate – no problem. Diary – I write in one occasionally to keep her happy if she snoops, kind of like a decoy. Cigarettes – she already knows about those. What else? What else?

I stop in the doorway. My room is perfectly tidy, not a book or a CD or a stuffed toy out of place. Just as I left it. I prowl, pulling open drawers and cupboards. It has to be something accidental, something I've forgotten about because I didn't think it was important, just a laugh or a curiosity thing.

Oh. Now I remember. No wonder she… It's the condoms. Black, super-sized, ribbed. I bought them last week to make water balloons out of them. I laugh. She thinks I'm having sex. If it wasn't so mortally serious, I'd die laughing. Who'd be desperate enough to want sex with me?

She won't believe a word I say, I know. Dad might, but he doesn't stick up for me much any more. If Mother's causing a huge fuss, he kind of shrinks away, usually to his office or to golf. When she's raving on about me, he hardly ever defends me. I hate that.

Now though, I reckon I'm screwed. Going back to Barton will kill me. White shirts, brown skirts, black lace-up shoes and brown socks. Hair tied back neatly. Punctuality. Discipline. Homework. Aaarrrgh!

But I know she's got me this time. When she says remedial boarding school, she means it. I ignore the dinner bell and fall onto my bed, wondering if I can smother myself with my own pillow. It seems a very tempting option.

I decide I'd better do the dinner thing so as not to make things worse. This entails dressing in something that won't freak my mother out too much, eating nicely with the correct cutlery, not talking to Nancy while she serves up the food, and only speaking when spoken to. Anything I do say needs to be intelligent, articulate and not some kind of smartarse retort. It'll be a good test for me. Fail right here, right now, and I've got no hope at all.

I don't own a dress that I'd be seen dead in, so I dig out a pair of black stretch pants and a plain white shirt. There's no time to remove studs or purple hair dye. I settle for scrubbing my face until it's all fresh and

pink. God, I must be desperate. I run down
the stairs, into the dining room and dive into
my chair, whip the starched napkin onto my
lap and place my hands on top, neatly folded.
Mother's face looks a picture of displeasure,
like she's a Victorian matron. It takes every
bit of control I can muster not to laugh. I
come close to exploding, then I bite the inside
of my mouth until I get it contained.

Nancy doesn't help. When I finally risk a
glance at her as she's ladling out some kind
of soup, her right eye is twitching so bad that
I think she's going to slop some of it down the
front of Mother's dress. I grab a dinner roll
and pull it apart, shredding it into crumbs.

Louise sits opposite Mother, rabbiting
on about some new CD she's bought that
has 'the most divine flute solo'. The soup
appears in the bowl in front of me looking
like green slime – I'm almost too scared to
taste it. Would my mother poison me?

Nah, Nancy wouldn't be up for that. Still,
it looks fairly gruesome. I lift a spoonful to
my mouth and taste it. Not bad. Creamy

and garlicky. I won't ask what the green is. Probably spinach.

I don't have the honour of being directly addressed until Mother has nearly finished her chicken breast and avocado with snap peas (we're definitely having a green night). She and Louise have talked about classical music, a new designer boutique that's opening on Saturday, and the maths teacher at Barton who Louise thinks is gay, though how she'd know is beyond me. She still thinks a dyke is a seawall in Holland. So when Mother actually says something to me, I nearly jump out of my fresh, white shirt.

'Huh?' I can see that's impressed her.

'I said, were you in detention again today, Deborah?' Her lemon-sucking mouth tells me she already knows that I was.

'Um, yes. Just a misunderstanding.'

'Oh?' She raises her eyebrows. She doesn't really care, she just wants to make me squirm.

'I... um... happened to be...' Oh, what's the use? She'll know I'm lying if I make something up. 'I refused to do PE yesterday and I didn't have a note.'

'PE? In what way?'

'They were showing everyone how to vault a horse and hang on those ring things. I said I'd sit that class out and the teacher got tetchy with me.'

Actually, I'd told *Feeble* that 'horse' was a dirty word to me and I'd rather clean toilets than jump on, over, or under the stupid contraption. His face turned almost terracotta and he actually spat on me when he ordered me to sit on the bench.

'Has your teacher not been advised of your *limitations*?' Mother frowns at me and pushes away her plate. By *limitations*, she means that my shoulder and arm still haven't healed properly. The school was supposed to have received a letter from my specialist, describing my injuries in great detail, and which activities I am not allowed to participate in. I know this because I ripped it up then burned it.

'I guess not. It's no big deal.' Oops, wrong thing to say. Now I get the frown and the lemon-lips together.

'Another good reason why that school is inadequate for your needs.'

Louise can't help herself. 'Ms Sharp asked me yesterday when you were coming back to Barton.' For sure, she knows what Mother's up to and she wants to turn the screw. 'She said the classical guitar group just isn't the same without you.'

I try to glare down the table at Mother but she turns away to talk to Nancy.

'I think we'll just have fruit salad and coffee, Nancy. I need to watch my weight a little more closely.'

As if! Mother is so skinny, her collar bones look like dinosaur fossils and her breasts are little saggy sacks. I burst in on her one day when she was dressing in the cabana by the pool. Man, was that a shock. No, this fruit salad thing is a dig at me, at the fact that although I'm still wearing the black clothes I bought last year in my first stages of *Up Yours, Mother*, large parts of me now bulge out over waistbands, split sleeves and stretch-pants legs.

'May I fetch the double choc-chip ice-cream?' I ask as nicely as possible.

That's got her. She wants to say no, but I know she's also made some kind of pact with herself not to criticise me about anything to do with my body. It's because of my shoulder and arm, of course, but extends to my former dancer's figure. Slim, trim and fighting fit. Now I'm just fighting.

She nods like her neck is in a brace and I head for the freezer in the kitchen, as Nancy emerges through the swing door, carrying a Wedgwood bowl of fresh fruit salad. When I bring the ice-cream back to the table, it's too much for Louise. She has to have some too. Mother spoons her fruit into her mouth like it's got worms in it.

I don't want coffee. I'm wired enough already, trying to be *good daughter number three* without cracking up. Now I'll pretend I'm having an early night and hide out in my room until Dad gets home. I really hope he'll listen. I don't want to think about all the other times in the past few years that he's quietly crept away from the Dragon Queen. I used to be his favourite, the one he'd always stick up for. What happened?

CHAPTER 5
Melissa

The alarm brrr-ings me awake at 6am. I whack the button so hard that I knock the clock off the side table. I don't want to get up. My knee and my elbow ached all night and kept me awake. Now I feel rotten.

Mrs Wyatt will be in around 7.30am to check on us. She nearly cried when she saw us hunched up against the front door last night. I felt awful upsetting her like that, but her son Bobby was great, just lifted Mum straight up and carried her to bed.

The twenty Bandaids Mrs Wyatt plastered on my knee and elbow feel like great wads of parcel tape. I can't go to school like this, but what's the alternative? Take them off and bleed everywhere? Maybe I'll have to go and see the first aid teacher before class. There's no time to worry about it now. I've got to get Mum showered, dressed and off to work. Plus coax some food into her – that's the most important thing.

She's hard to wake but I get the routine going. Turn on the shower, pull the blankets off, stand her up, then nudge her under the water. Ten minutes usually does it. By then she's awake and can shampoo and wash on her own. I lay out clean clothes, make breakfast. Today she can have the omelette she missed out on.

'Hey, Melissa, this is great. I'm so hungry.' She sits down without looking at me. I know she's ashamed.

'Eat up, Mum. I'll make us some lunch, then you'd better get going.' I'm not going to ask one question about her new job in case she starts talking about Gordon. Instead I put a piece of paper and a pen next to her plate. She writes down the name of the company and contact details. I wave her off before hunting around for something to wear to school, something not too worn or daggy, something that turns me into wallpaper. My maths books sit beside my bed, shouting *Guess what you didn't do last night!* Shit. Homework. Maths is second period. Maybe I can do it during English.

This hour of peace and space after Mum leaves keeps me sane. I love her heaps, but this time is mine. It's like a little bird takes flight inside me when she goes. I feel guilty about that for a moment or two, but the time is too precious to waste. I have my shower, wander around naked, sing, write poems, listen to the tiny radio on the windowsill. I sit by the window, watching the busy bugs below all hurrying along to their jobs, imagining myself doing exactly the same thing one day. Maybe I'll work in an office, or a shop. I'd really love to be a nurse, but that seems way out of reach right now. I don't let myself dream *that* dream very often.

I'm feeling a bit antsy about this detention thing. It hangs around in the back of my head,

interrupting the good thoughts. I don't want
to be late for school. God, what if they added
to my detention? I really would kill Dobie.
I haven't forgotten the fire hose thing. She
knew it was me coming around that corner. I
still don't know what was more embarrassing
– being soaked by the hose or having to strip
off in the first aid room and Ms Rogers staring
at my tatty old bra and pants. I could tell she
felt sorry for me, but she didn't have to offer
me money to buy new ones. I wanted to run
home right away. Except I had no clothes on.

I'm getting totally pissed off. I have to
stop thinking about all this or I'll lose it
again. A picture of the principal's face pops
into my mind, how his mouth fell open when
I called him a stupid, bum-faced shit-for-
brains. Mum used to say, 'Close your mouth
before you catch a fly.' He would've caught
a whole bunch of them! God, no wonder I
ended up in detention.

My knee seems OK so I leave two
Bandaids on it. I pick out an old pair of
jeans and a black T-shirt with a dog on the
front. It labels me *dork* quite nicely.

I'm halfway to school, a new poem just starting to simmer in my head, when I hear something squeaking. It sounds like an injured bird, one of those brown things that steals food from all the other birds. Probably nearly dead, too far gone. If I try to help it, I'll only make it worse. I hear it cry again. Maybe it's not a bird after all. The noise is coming from behind a pile of rubbish bins next to an old apartment building streaked with rust stains. A newspaper item flashes in my brain: *Teen mother leaves newborn in dumpster*. Whoa, it can't be a baby. That's just me being over the top.

I try to keep walking, but my feet won't move along the street. Instead they take me over to the bins. The smell is like rotten cheese, so bad I want to gag. I swallow hard and peer around the bins, holding my breath.

There, huddled into a little black furball, is a kitten. It opens its mouth wide and another wail dribbles from its pink throat.

'Oh no, buddy, you're on your own there. Don't look at me to save you.' It gazes up at me like it's hoping for its mother. 'I've gotta get to school. Detention. No time for cats.' I walk away, but I'm back within twenty seconds. I did at least make it as far as the pavement.

As soon as I pick it up, the problems start. It's so skinny that its ribs feel like toothpicks. Millions of fleas crawl through its fur, and one jumps onto my hand straight away. 'Gross!' I flick it off, hold the kitten at arm's length and jog back to our flat. There's no time to get all gooey over it. I peel off a few feet of toilet paper, grab our rag towel out of the cupboard and dump the kitten in the bathtub along with the last of our milk in a bowl. 'You're lucky I didn't have cereal this morning, kitty.' A quick scrub of my hands gets rid of the crawly feeling. Now I have to run at top speed to get to school in time.

I just about make it, though I'm hot and sweaty. My heart's pounding with either relief or imminent heart attack at all this running. First period is English; by the time Ms Rogers has read another few pages of *Wuthering Heights* and asked some questions that no one bothers to answer, I've calmed down. I can feel her eyes on me. Sometimes it's like she knows I know the answers to all the stuff she asks us and it's got her really puzzled as to why I never put up my hand.

It's hard not to. I used to be a top student, all As, especially in English. I bet I've read books that would surprise Ms Rogers. Dad had this huge library in his study, all those leather-bound classics just for show that no one ever actually opened. *Anna Karenina* and *David Copperfield* were my favourites, but I also got into *The Fountainhead* and other modern classics. Sometimes I was tempted to write notes in the books or leave clues that I'd been there but in the end I decided it wasn't worth it. They'd never be found.

All through class I keep thinking about the kitten. Mum is going to freak. There's no way I'll give it a name. That's asking for trouble. What if we have to move again? I'd have to get it put down. That would be almost as bad as ...

Sometimes that day comes back to me so vividly it's like watching myself in a home movie. I'd skipped school for the day because it was boiling hot and I felt a bit sick every time I went outside. I lay on the couch, half-listening to the little black and white TV until nearly midday, then dug out the ice-cream from the freezer and scooped some into a bowl. That little house Mum and I had in that town always stank of dogs and disinfectant in the heat. It was the second place we'd run to, all the way across the country this time, and we were getting poorer. I opened all the windows to make up for the dead air conditioner. Mum had said maybe next payday she could afford to get it fixed.

I sat in the old wicker chair by the big front window, leaning against the sill, picking bits of peeling paint off the wood as I ate my ice-cream and watched Mrs Miller across the road. She lay back in an old plastic lounge chair on her front porch, yelling every now and then at her two little kids who were using the derelict pink Chevrolet on the front lawn as a playground.

Tiny George liked to sit in the front on a box and tug at the steering wheel, pretending he was driving somewhere exciting.

I heard the music first, and couldn't quite remember for a moment what it reminded me of. Then the hammer fell and I pulled back from the window really fast, hiding behind the tatty curtain.

It wasn't a car I recognised, but I knew it all the same. Dad always bought something flash and expensive. When Mum and I left, it'd been a Mercedes. This was a bright red Jaguar, the silver cat on the bonnet leaping forward, aggressive. The music hadn't changed. Country and western – old whiney songs about lost love and broken down trucks that set my teeth on edge. 'I cain't le-er-rve no one else but yoooo...'

The Jag pulled up at the kerb opposite the house next door. I held my breath and waited, wanting desperately to run, but wanting even more to see what he would do. He climbed out of the car and looked around, his lip curling. Definitely not his kind of neighbourhood. He spotted Mrs Miller and strolled across to stand next to the pink Chev.

I was so used to being suspicious of everyone that I was just waiting for her to spill her guts to Dad. Hell, he'd probably offer her money – that was his style.

Tiny George had spotted Dad and honed in on his neatly pressed trouser leg, wiping his sticky hands on the material and probably his snotty nose too. Good one, Tiny George. Mrs Miller didn't even bother to raise her head from the lounger. She shaded her eyes, shook her head and waved her hand towards the other end of the street.

I knew that wouldn't fool Dad for a minute, but she was a honey for doing it. I didn't wait any longer. I didn't even stop long enough to pack my few things worth taking. I grabbed my school backpack, slipped out the back door, leaving the whole house wide open, and ran for my life. Four blocks away, inside a noisy supermarket, I found a payphone and rang Mum at work.

Like me, she grabbed her bag and left. She picked me up at the edge of the park where I was waiting just inside the entrance to the stinking public toilets. It was another week before Mrs Miller and Mum thought it was safe enough for Mrs Miller to go into our house and pack up what was left to send to us. *What was left* was a pretty good description. When Dad had finally worked out that he'd only missed us by minutes, he'd gone into the house and trashed it. All of our clothes were ripped up, my books torn apart, and the furniture smashed to pieces. Since it came with the rental of the house, we'd lost our bond. Another eight hundred dollars down the tubes.

Mrs Miller tried to patch up my old brown bear for me before she sent it on, but I could see where his legs and arms had been severed and a big hole punched in the back of his head. I couldn't stand to have him around any more, but I cried my eyes out when I stuck him in the bin.

So now I'm sitting in maths class with tears in my eyes, staring down at the same old algebra problems, wondering how long it'll be before Mum and I have to take off again. I think of the kitten instead, pretending it really is going to be all mine, trying to work out what would be the best thing to put in the wash water to kill all those fleas.

'Melissa? Have you finished Exercise 22?'

'No, Mr Canto.' I haven't even started it.

'Did you do your homework?' His tone has got that little edge to it.

Shit. Detention. I want to leap right out of my skin, my nerves are jumping around so bad. 'Uh, no, I, uh, couldn't figure out how.'

'Really. We have spent the whole week on this particular type of problem. Did you have some kind of mental blockage?'

He smirks, his grey moustache flexing, and suddenly I see how easy it would be to become Dobie Lessing. To tell some of these smartarse teachers to go jump off a high cliff. I settle for a lie. I'm good at them. 'I haven't been feeling very well, sir. Shall I get my mother to write a note for me?' I force out a greasy smile that nearly kills me.

'That won't be necessary. If you continue to have trouble, maybe you'd better come in at lunchtime and I'll give you some extra exercises.'

For sure he knows that I'm already on detention. He's just saying this to needle me. I say, 'That's OK, I think I've nearly got it now.'

'Make sure you do, Melissa. We have a test on Monday.'

He turns away just in time to catch two of the boys at the back of the room playing with their little rubber catapults, pelting people with wads of paper. In an instant, I'm small potatoes and can relax.

But it's reminded me that I have to report to the detention room again this afternoon. My heart scrunches up when I think of the kitten mewing in the bath tub all day, starving while I sit in that smelly little room with Dobie. I don't allow myself to wonder if Mum will be home on time today. For once, I manage to block her out completely.

CHAPTER 6
Dobie

The only thing that propels me out of bed this morning is the thought that if I stop going to Village Gate High School, I will have absolutely no excuse at all for not going back to Barton. I sit on the end of my bed, staring at all the grungy black clothes hanging in my walk-in closet. I hate every item in there.

Last year when I bought it all, it was fun. I never realised how many things you could buy in black. I felt like I was stocking up for the world's largest funeral. And wishing it was my mother's funeral. I told myself I didn't miss my bright pink shirt or my favourite summer skirt with the blue

flowers on it that swirled around my ankles.
I made myself give all those kinds of clothes
away to the church shop so if Mum came
snooping, she wouldn't think I was *just
going through a stage.*

But now most of it doesn't fit properly
and black is pretty good at fading to a dull,
dirty grey. One more day in those heavy
boots, dragging my feet along brown-tiled
corridors, and my legs will drop off. Trouble
is, I don't have any choice. The one possibility
is to sneak into Louise's or Sara's room and
borrow something. Not likely. If I turned
up at Village Gate in a straight skirt and
cashmere sweater, they'd laugh me out of
the classroom.

I pull on my stretchiest pair of black
jeans and my baggiest T-shirt, run my
fingers through my hair. Yuck, it's oily
and stiff at the same time. It's a wonder it
doesn't all just fall out.

Nancy's made me a sandwich that I
collect on my way through the kitchen, along
with a snack bar for my breakfast. I eat it

on the bus while I keep thinking about the school problem. I hate, hate, hate the way my mother has manipulated this whole thing. The smouldering coals that are always in my stomach have been fanned into flames that leap up and turn my face hot. The only solution is to make Village Gate sound like such a wonderful school that I can't bear to leave. Mission Impossible.

My brain grinds back and forth between Barton and Village Gate, trying to find some way of making the Gate sound good. But I've already shot myself in the foot by causing so much trouble and being in detention four days out of five. And I have to admit (through clenched teeth) that Mother is right in one respect – the teachers and the subjects offered at the Gate are pitiful.

Maybe a boarding school mightn't be so bad. No, trash that thought! Mother would make sure it was like a prison. Education be damned.

I want to jump up on the bus seat and kick out the emergency window, scream at everyone on the street, 'Help me! My mother is killing me!' Then they really would send me away.

In English, I sit at the back and glare at the boys who are stabbing each other under the desks with their rulers. Why doesn't Ms Rogers do something about it? She reads *Wuthering Heights* like the end of the world is coming. Someone needs to tell her that she's living a ridiculous dream. She'd be a good teacher at Barton. Here she's just spinning her wheels in the mud.

One of the boys, Spike Donivan, catches my glare, leans over and asks me if I want a fuck later in the boys' changing room. As if! I give him the look I've been perfecting on my mother for the past year or two and he withers.

In maths, Mr Canto picks on Goody. For just one second, I think she's going to tell him where to stick his homework, then she buckles under and grovels so bad I want to hit her. Dad would say she needs a bit more 'gumption'. She sure needs something.

I waited for hours last night for Dad to come home. Sara arrived from her choir practice about nine and Mother insisted on hearing her sing the new song they're learning for the mid-year concert. She sounded squeaky and out of tune to me, but that might be the little green monster jumping inside my head. He's dangerous – he makes me want things I will never have.

I sneaked downstairs after everyone else had gone to bed and curled up on the big armchair in his study. Dad always stops in there for a scotch before going to bed, no matter how late it is. He didn't see me, just headed for the bar and jumped about a foot off the ground when I said *hi*. As soon as he turned around, I saw that look on his face, the one that says *Don't serve me up any more trouble, my plate is already full.*

Yeah, but what about me, Dad?

He listened to everything I said about Mother and the school, giving his head a little shake every so often like he was trying not to let any of my complaints lodge in there permanently. Then he shrugged. *Shrugged!* 'Your mother is just worried about you, Deb,' he said. 'I am too, you know. You're a bright girl. You know I have nothing against state schools but Village Gate is hardly going to extend you academically. Don't you miss your music?'

I wasn't going to be sidetracked that easily. 'Barton is narrow-minded and bigoted. What about all the stuff you've said to me about the right to think independently and not follow the herd?'

'Deb, you could make a difference in the world. You understand issues and you want to fight to make things right. Sara and Louise will never achieve that, they won't even want to. Why are you wasting your energy and talents on paying back your mother? Even if she deserved it, and I'm not sure she does, it's a waste of *you*.'

I couldn't believe he was sticking up for her! I was so angry with him, I could've spat on him. 'You don't understand the first

thing about me. If you loved me, you'd stop
her from doing this.' I was shouting, but I
couldn't help it.

He didn't even try to argue. He just gave
that stupid shrug and went back to the bar
to pour himself a drink. I wanted to tell him
I hoped he choked on it, but suddenly it was
like he'd moved a thousand miles away from
me, across a huge canyon. I wasn't even sure
I could see him clearly any more. I stalked
out of the study and ran up the stairs. Mother
was standing in the doorway of her bedroom,
pulling on her red velvet dressing gown.
I stepped around her, went into my room and
locked the door, rattling the catch to make
sure she heard it and got the message.

I watch Canto trying to discipline
the ferals who are firing paper pellets at
people. Why doesn't he just send them out
of the room? I keep my fingers crossed that
he doesn't end up giving them detention.
Goody McCardle is bad enough.

Canto spots me watching and sidles over
to give me a hard time.

'Exercise 22 giving you trouble too, Deborah?'

I don't bother to answer, just shove my notebook across the desk at him. My handwriting is scrawly, but I've done all the problems *and* got them right. Usually, if I do anything I deliberately get it wrong. His mouth opens but he can't think of anything to say. Score one for me! He gives me a funny look and walks back to the front of the classroom.

Detention on Friday is always boring. All the teachers leave as soon as they can, some of them actually run to their cars. Can't blame them. But there's no one to eavesdrop on, and half the time it ends up being the principal who has to supervise me. That's a drag because he always finds chores for me to do. One time it was filing, another time it was washing all the leaves on the ugly rubber plants in the teachers' lounge and his office.

My brain hurries back to the problem of schools like a dog digging up the same old dead cat in the back yard. I wonder how much time I've got before Mother puts her plan into action and pulls me out of here. Will being a good girl here make any difference? I can't decide. Besides, getting up the teachers' noses and squashing bugs like Spike Donivan is fun in a sick kind of way. When I make them back down or I see that uncertainty in their eyes, it cools the burning down a little bit and makes me feel taller and stronger. And just a tiny bit like I used to feel when I was dancing, spinning and leaping across the floor, the whole world inside me bursting to expand.

Shit! I promised myself I wouldn't go there. That's not a place I belong any more and it hurts too much. I don't want to remember what it was like. I'll never, ever have it again. I have to keep it as far away as possible, obliterate it. One day it will just be something I enjoyed when I was younger, something not very important, a little hobby.

OK, so the me I am now is a Gate student, a troublemaker, a regular in detention, a person who hates everyone around her. I'm not suddenly going to turn into Goody McCardle. Mother wouldn't care anyway. She'd just see it as a sign I was ready to be a Barton girl again.

Back to where I started from. Stuck. Up against the wall. Stymied. Trapped. Losing the war.

CHAPTER 7
Melissa

The library at lunchtime would have to be the quietest place in the whole school. I sit at the long table next to the dictionaries and encyclopaedias and try to finish all of my maths. Last night's homework, tonight's homework and that scummy Exercise 22.

I draw little boxes around the numbers and letters in the algebra problem but it doesn't help; a is being ridiculous today, trying to tell me it's equal to about a thousand when I know b is worth 11. Can't work out y. It's wriggling around on the page, won't stay in one place. Maybe y has fleas, like that kitten.

What would be a great name for a kitten like that? Blackie? Boring. Midnight? That's more like it. It probably would be OK to wash it in detergent, if I didn't get any in its eyes. It. I don't even know if it's a boy or a girl. Not that it matters. I can't keep it.

In fifth period, Ms Mitchell tries hard to get everyone excited about Abraham Lincoln and presidential power, but she doesn't get anyone to pay attention until she talks about his assassination. She says, 'Would you call John Wilkes Booth a terrorist or just a murderer?'

Some hands actually spring up like daffodils from the mud. Man, one of them is Dobie's. I sit up and listen. This could be interesting.

She's obviously given Ms Mitchell a shock too. 'Er, yes, Deborah, what do you think?'

'Terrorist is a totally over-used term, and it is usually used inappropriately anyway, especially by the media. The correct word for a political murderer is assassin.' Dobie's voice is calm, like she's giving a lecture at a museum or something. The other kids glance at each other and raise their eyebrows, and some boys go, 'Oooooohhh,' but Dobie's right.

'Er, yes, you're probably correct.' Ms Mitchell is struggling for an answer. 'However, if we think about what terrorists in today's world try to achieve, how their beliefs make them think *they* are in the right, can we compare that to Booth?'

'Booth was part of a political movement, but in the end he's remembered more as an insane individual. Isn't terrorism more about using violence and killing to inflict your obsessions on other people?' Dobie hasn't bothered to put her hand up. She says what she wants, then sits back in her chair as if she's waiting to see how many angry ants she's stirred up.

Heaps. A dozen hands waggle in the air and Ms Mitchell looks quite excited. This is the most interest this class has shown in weeks.

Belinda gets in first as usual. Her ponytail bobs around when she talks. 'I think all the terrorists are insane individuals. They just use their religion as an excuse.'

It's never that simple. Look at Dad. In our town he was Mr Charity. Gave heaps of money to the hospital and had an ECG machine named after him. Senior partner in a big law firm. Ran a very efficient debt collection business on the side. I guess he still does. Mum and I skipping out on him must have dented his reputation a little bit, but no doubt he made up some story that turned Mum into a raving loony.

'Melissa, what do you think?' Ms Mitchell is beaming at me like she thinks I'm about to say something highly intelligent. Why on earth do the teachers always pick on me to answer questions? I sit here minding my own business, being anonymous, and they turn me into teacher's suck.

'I think Dobie's right. Lots of people are terrorists, even the people we live with every day. If you're trying to kill someone or make their life not worth living just because you've got lots of power, then you're a terrorist too.' Oops, where did that come from? I should've kept my big mouth shut. Funny thing though – some of the girls are nodding like they know exactly what I'm talking about.

'I totally agree with that.' Dobie's still lounging back in her chair, but she's scowling big time.

Mitchell looks at her for a couple of seconds. She opens her mouth then shuts it again, like she was going to say something.

Instead she glances down at the book in her hand and says, 'So what about Booth?'

Mitchell's destroyed the whole thing we were getting into. Dobie's mouth twists. She obviously thinks Mitchell's a chicken, like I do. I wanted to hear what else Dobie might say. Why would she agree with me? What would she know?

Next period is P.E. in the gym. Shit. I hate the gym, and I especially hate it right now.

That vaulting horse looks about ten feet high to me. How can I get out of it? Fake rabies? Faint?

Some of the kids are already lined up for the horse. They actually like bouncing on that stupid little springboard and sailing up into the air. I want to keep my feet on the ground. Dobie didn't get changed and Feibler's sent her back, no excuses accepted unless you have a note. I should've faked one for myself.

She comes back out and stands, arms crossed; her bottom lip sticking out. Feibler's not happy either.

'There's nothing to be scared of. If you take it slowly, you'll soon get the hang of it. Look at the others.'

'I'm not scared. I just won't do it, that's all.' Dobie points past the mats. 'What about that? Why can't I do that?'

I look to where she's pointing. It's a long piece of wood, raised about a foot off the floor.

'The beam? Bit tame for you, isn't it?' Feibler shrugs. 'Fine, do that then. As long as you're doing something. I'll come and give you some help in a minute.' He glares around at everyone who's not running, jumping or swinging on a piece of equipment. Basically, that means me.

'Miss McCardle, join Miss Lessing on the beam. I imagine the horse is beyond you as well?'

He's being sarcastic, but that's OK. If I don't have to jump over that monstrous thing, I don't care what he says. Except now I'm stuck with Dobie again. It's like a curse. By the time I get over to the beam, she's up on it, balancing on one foot, her other one up in the air. She'd look like a ballerina if she was skinnier. She leans forward and her leg goes straight up, toes pointed. Maybe she does do ballet.

Just as I open my mouth to ask, she lowers her leg and jumps off.

'Your turn. You'll have to take your runners off.'

The cool, dusty floor under my feet reminds me of my naked dances in the mornings. My face gets hot and I step onto the beam too quickly. Straight away, I overbalance and have to jump off. I don't look to see if she's laughing. I bite my lip and step on again, more carefully this time. The beam seems wide and solid but once I'm on it, it's suddenly narrow. I have to keep one foot in front of the other.

'Find your centre, down in your guts. Take a deep breath and focus. Don't think about your feet or you'll never stay on.' It's Dobie, giving me instructions. She sounds like an expert, encouraging and firm; I take a breath and let it out, wondering where on earth my centre is. But then I feel something settle in the pit of my stomach like an anchor on the sea bed so I focus on that and ignore my feet, like she said.

'Centre your weight over your right foot and lift the left. Slowly.'

But she just told me to ignore my feet! My right one's at the back. The anchor shifts back a little, I raise my left foot, bending my knee. I get it up about nine inches. Hey, maybe I could be the next Karate Kid! Uh oh, a big wobble sets in and I fall off.

'Lost your focus, huh?' Dobie hops up on the beam. She makes it look like it's about two feet wide. 'Takes a while to get it. You lasted longer than I thought you would.'

Who the hell does she think she is? Every day she's Bad Attitude to the extreme, now she's Beam Queen. But I can't help watching closely as she balances, stretches, swings around, does these ballet poses like she was born to it.

'Hey, you're really good. Do you learn ballet or something?'

That makes her wobble for a few seconds until she gets it under control. Her face has gone all dark and she's probably going to tell me to piss off, or worse, but she doesn't.

'I used to.' She points down at the beam. 'The best gymnasts can turn somersaults on this thing, you know.'

'Are you going to try it?' That'd be amazing. I bet she could do it, too.

'Nah. Can't.'

'Oh.' I don't know what else to add. There's something about the way she said 'Can't' that felt loaded, like she meant stuff way beyond me. I'm not going to pry.

Feibler comes over to order us around but he stops when he sees Dobie balancing with her eyes closed. She doesn't know he's there and she does that leg thing again, getting it nearly perpendicular, her arms out like bird wings. Feibler watches her for two or three minutes and shakes his head. By the time she opens her eyes, he's gone back to the kids on the horse.

'Feibler came over. He was watching you,' I tell her.

'I know. I could smell him. Last period he's always sweaty and he sprays on more deodorant.' She grins. 'Come on, your turn. Have to make it look good so he won't decide you need a turn on the horse.'

This time I raise one leg behind me and spread my arms. When I start to wobble, Dobie steadies me with two fingers on my shoulder. 'Breathe and centre,' is all she says, and when the anchor settles again, she takes her hand away. I'm breathing slowly, lifting my leg, stretching forward. I could balance here for hours, I think, until my standing leg gets a major wobble and I have to step down to the floor. Back to reality.

I look up and Dobie's smiling this huge smile. It's so unlike her that I'm speechless. 'That was amazingly good for a first-timer,' she says, and now I'm so astonished, I have to sit down.

CHAPTER 8
Dobie

Today, for the first time since the accident, I felt like air. Balanced, free, in that space that I only used to find in dancing. I thought I'd lost it forever. We didn't do much beam work at Barton, and only a little bit in dance class, but I'd forgotten the simple gut-level stuff that happens when you focus like that.

Marveen talked about it sometimes. She'd phrase it like a lecture but she was really trying to get everyone to come together in that central place. She'd quote this poem by Yeats, *The Second Coming*, about things falling apart and the centre not being able to hold. Something like that. When I went and looked it up to read the whole thing, I didn't understand it. Still don't, but I like the lines.

God, how long is it since I allowed myself to think of Marveen? Or the dance classes? Even when I was mobile again and my arm was out of that straitjacket sling, I couldn't go back, not even to say *hi*. Seeing the others leaping around the floor, especially the hopeless ones who couldn't even keep time properly, would've killed me.

Couldn't do it. Don't even want to think about it.

Goody surprised me. She was a bit awkward but she managed the centring and balance thing like she'd been doing it for years. Well, maybe she has, but I don't think so. She doesn't seem the type to dance or play music or anything like that. Except for her poems.

Goody got a note to see the principal just before class finished. What was that about? Wonder if she'll tell me. I've been waiting in detention for ten minutes and no one's turned up. The smell today is vomitous. Maybe someone did vomit in here.

The door opens with a snap like the person on the other side is trying to rip the handle off. It's Goody, with a face like God having a bad sinners' day. Mr Hornsby is right behind her. That explains a lot.

'God helps those who help themselves, Ms McCardle,' Hornsby says, in a tone that makes me want to grab him by his big red nose and twist it until he begs for mercy. I take back what I said about Goody's face. She's not God, she's the sinner. I swear I can hear her teeth grinding from here.

'Yes, sir.' Goody is grovelling; I want to shake her, make her stick up for herself, then I hear her mutter, 'Stupid prick,' and I have to duck my head. Hornsby can't decide whether he heard what she said correctly, but in the end he ignores it.

'You girls are here until five. I will be back to check on you. If you're not using your time constructively, I shall have to find chores for you to do.' He sniffs and leaves, closing the door behind him like it's really made of iron bars.

So, no tree washing or filing today. Hmmm, homework. Now there's a novel idea. Goody drags her books out of her bag, sits down and puts her head on the top book, jamming her fingers in her ears. I sit back in my chair and watch her. There's not much else to do and I figure she's got to come up for air sooner or later.

It takes a few minutes. I'm starting to get bored, thinking about sneaking out for a walk, when she sighs and straightens up. There's a possibility she was crying but her face is dry and looks like a papier-mâché mask.

'What do you think of Ms Rogers?' she says to the ceiling. 'Apart from the fact that she's an interfering cow.'

Does she want an answer? 'She's OK. Wasted here. Can't cope with all the kids who don't want to be here.'

'Like you?'

'I didn't say I didn't want to be here.'

'You don't work in class, don't say anything unless you have to, don't do homework, spend your time finding new ways to get detention.' She turns to look at me, a funny little smile trying to turn her mouth up again. 'I'd nominate you for Student of the Year ahead of Spike Donivan, but that's about all.'

'This school has Student of the Year?' I'm astounded. Look what I've been missing out on.

'Are you kidding? Course not.' Goody laughs but it sounds rusty at first until she gets the hang of it, then she can't stop. I have to laugh at her laughing, even if she is a bit hysterical. Then it's all over and she sighs, tapping her fingers on her books.

'Algebra. Last week, easy-peasy. This week, gibberish.'

'Canto. Last week, Mr Nice. This week, the Hound from Hell. What's the problem?'

'System error. I think my hard drive has crashed.' She taps her head.

'You want some help?' As soon as it's out of my mouth, I wish I could call it back. I don't want to be anyone's buddy, helper, saviour.

She giggles again. 'You've failed every maths test this term. I don't need help in how *not* to do it.'

She's saying I'm stupid! Ignorant cow. 'I failed those tests on purpose.'

'What for? What's the point?'

She doesn't believe me, I can tell. 'The point is my mother. She put me here to teach me a lesson. So I'm teaching her one back.'

She sort of shakes her head, like I'm speaking a foreign language. I turn my back to her and pull some books out of my bag. No way I'm doing any homework but if Hornsby comes back, I can look busy in a second.

Then, just when I thought I'd squashed it back into its hole, the horrible, black nothingness of my life zooms out and smothers me. I have to fight to get a breath, I know my fingers are pulling at my clothes but I can't stop them. *Count, count, COUNT, one two three, light in, black out, four five six, light in, black out...*

Suddenly hands are on my head, not the cold ones; warm, quiet, resting, these are. Someone's behind me, leaning me back into their body, warm hands holding. I breathe, count, breathe. The black thing slides back into its hole. I open my eyes, it's so bright that I have to blink hard.

It's Goody behind me. Shit! Get me away from her. I jump up from my chair, head for the door, open it and run. Down the shadowed corridor, past empty rooms, battered lockers, heading for the double doors where the sun is shining. I burst out through the doors, make it as far as a wooden seat by a weed-filled garden and sit down in a heap, my legs shaking.

I don't know what's worse – having one of my stupid freak-outs in front of Goody or having her feel sorry for me and touch me. No one touches me, *no one*.

Then she sits down next to me and I hold myself very tightly, getting it all under control. Just waiting for the sympathy, the sorry voice, the same old lines the shrink gave me that Mother picked up on, repeating them like some kind of magic mantra until I told her to shut up before I tore her limb from limb. Go on, Goody. Say your pity piece.

'You don't seem the type for drugs,' she says.

'Huh?'

'That's the easy way out, anyway. Only postpones the shit that's causing it all.' She leans back and puts her face up to the afternoon sun.

OK, I'll play along, but what could she really know? 'The shrink wanted to put me on tranquillisers for a while but I said no. Maybe I should say yes. What do you think? You sound like an expert.' Did she catch the sarcasm? I kept it minimal.

'Yeah, I am a bit. Say no. Better to face the dragon.'

'You've met my mother, have you? Tell me, what do you do with dragons that're undefeatable?'

'They're always in it to win, at all costs. And usually better at battle tactics. You have to be trickier, faster, plan your moves, like in chess. They're cunning with words too, and use them to try and crush resistance.'

I think about what she said, and something happens inside my head, like a door opening so that I catch a glimpse of sunlight.

'Um, I think maybe I've got two dragons. One inside and one outside. And I'm not sure which one is bigger and meaner.'

Ow! She's grabbed me by the arm and is dragging me back inside. 'Hornsby!' she hisses, 'Heading across from his office.' We start running, our feet thumping down the corridor. Too bad if he hears us. By the time he gets to the detention room, we'll be sitting like little mice, studying and finishing our homework. The Hornsby dragon is barely knee-high, easy to kick aside.

CHAPTER 9
Melissa

I'm still puffing a bit when Hornsby opens the door and peers in suspiciously, but it's more my red face I'm worried about. I keep my head down, pretending the algebra is so fascinating that I'm really on Planet Maths. He must've heard us running.

'Have you two left this room?'

Like we're going to admit it. I stare up at him, acting like I've only just realised he's there. 'Pardon, sir?'

'Perhaps I should sit in here and keep an eye on you.'

Hornsby's trying to sound in control but I can see his big nose twitching as he takes in the smell. He's not staying, no way. Sure enough, he rabbits on about detention teaching us blah blah blah, then he gets out before the smell chokes him.

I open my mouth to crack some joke about him but stop myself. I don't want to talk to Dobie right now. I put my head down again and glare at the algebra. There's a whole jumble of things in my head – her drenching me with the hose, her hate-filled face when she saw me in here yesterday, her smile when I balanced on the beam. Who is she? Which person is she? The one who thinks I'm scum, or the one who helped me? I can't afford to open up to someone like Dobie. What if she saw my mother in one of her demented times, shaking and crying and trying to hide in the wardrobe? She'd drop me like a hot biscuit.

See, now she's ignoring me. She doesn't know when she's well off. Never had to run from anything. Probably the only time she's ever been in hospital is to visit some relative.

The ER is the worst place, like some of the descriptions I've read of Hell. All these dying, injured bodies everywhere; people shouting and pushing trolleys; sitting in the hard, plastic chairs with the man next to you coughing his guts out, being told you'll have to wait because your mum's injuries aren't serious and they've just had a triple car pile-up in. I could write scripts for one of those TV shows.

I still remember Mum clinging to me, sobbing her heart out at the same time as she's saying, 'I'm OK, Lissy, let's just go home, I don't want to cause any bother,' while I'm fighting the urge to shake her until her head rattles clear and she sees what she's doing. Giving in again. Letting him get away with it. When we finally saw a doctor, she stitched up the cut on Mum's cheek, checked the huge lump on her head and tried to talk to her about reporting the attack, but Mum wouldn't listen. She kept shaking her head, then she said, 'I fell down the stairs.'

Yeah, well, she could tell herself the stairs story all she liked (she kept alternating that with the 'walked into a door' one) until the day Dad actually cut her with the hunting knife he kept in his desk drawer, sharpened like a meat worker's. He sliced a neat line across one breast, over her heart. That's when he told her that if she ever left, he'd finish the job by cutting her throat.

If he knew I listened outside their door, he probably would've said the same to me. But he always acted like he was the best father in the world. I had every toy I wanted, the latest fashions, big hugs all the time. It got so every time he cuddled me, I had to keep swallowing so as not to throw up.

After that first time in the ER, I had to eavesdrop. I knew Mum wouldn't protect herself. I had to do it. When he cut her breast, I nearly burst into the bedroom to try to kill him. I thought hard about the gun he hid in the drawer on his side of the bed, but I was pretty sure he didn't keep it loaded. After that, I couldn't get the knife out of my head. It's my fault we ran and it's me who has to keep Mum going, hold her up. If I let her down, she'll crumble and go back to him. And eventually she'll be dead.

There's a cracking, splintering noise and I look down at the pen in my hand, or what's left of it.

I shouldn't have said anything about dragons. What was I doing? Looking for sympathy?

I can feel Dobie watching me. Doesn't matter what she says, I'm going to shut her out. She'll soon get the message, then she'll go back to being horrible. That's safer, easier.

CHAPTER 10
Dobie

Something's changed. I can feel it, like something died in here and the smell's just got worse. Hey, Goody's just smashed her pen. Weird. Why did she do that? That algebra must really be getting to her. I could help, but... I don't do that kind of thing. Especially for someone as weedy as her. She always looks so pale and skinny. Must have a bit of strength, though. That pen is history.

'You want to borrow a pen?'

'No, thanks.'

Goody's acting like I offered her arsenic.

What is going on in her head? Man, it stinks in here!

I'll have a go at opening that miniscule window up there. I climb on a desk, flick the catch and push as hard as I can. It's stuck. Maybe if I thump it. It shudders and the paint along the sill cracks so I thump it harder and it moves. Some dickhead has painted it shut. By the time I finish pushing and banging, it's open about four inches. The glass is cracked, but that's too bad. I can actually smell fresh air seeping in.

I jump down off the desk, bending my knees to land, and hear a sound. Shit! I know exactly what's happened. I've split my jeans, right down the back seam. What undies did I put on today? Have to be black. Hope they're clean. For a second I hear Mother's voice saying, 'Diet, diet, diet.' If I ever get home without the whole world noticing and laughing themselves stupid, I'd better find a way to get up to my room without Mother seeing my cringing embarrassment. I haven't even got a sweatshirt I can tie around my waist.

'Um, you haven't got a sweatshirt in your locker, have you?' It's worth a try.

'No.'

Goody's either blind or she's pretending I don't exist again. 'What's your problem?' I ask, snappier than I planned.

'People bugging me.' Her voice sounds choked.

'Hey, I didn't ask you to be in here. You did that all on your own. Although how you'd have the guts to do anything worth a detention is beyond me.'

'What would you know? You don't know anything. Little rich girl playing stupid games. You wouldn't know real life if it walked up and spat in your face.'

Her face has gone red and her eyes are all dark and glittery. God, what if she ups and hits me?

'You don't know anything about me –' I

start, but she cuts in.

'And you don't know anything about me, so butt out!'

One part of me is really mad at her, but another part is suddenly curious. She's so useless most of the time, then she turns into this fiery monster. I think about what she just said and start laughing.

'Butt out, that's great. That's exactly what I've done, my butt's hanging out in a big way.' It's not that funny but laughing helps whatever is going on here. I turn around and show her my jeans. When I turn back she's trying hard not to smile. At least she's polite.

CHAPTER 11

Melissa

I can't help it, I have to laugh. How embarrassing. I'd die if it was me. Dobie swings her bum around like she doesn't care. When she smiles like that, it's infectious; I have to smile too, even if I don't want to.

'My sweatshirt's at home. Sorry.'

'That's OK, maybe I can walk all the way home like this.' She squeezes her bum in and waddles around the room.

It won't hurt to be a little bit nice to her, I guess. After all, we've got another day in here yet. It's nearly 4.30, only half an hour to go. I suddenly think about the kitten crying in the bathtub, Mum coming home and finding it, and I'm itching to get out of here. 'You think Hornsby will come back again?'

'For sure. Mrs Gregson has gone home so he'll waste time annoying us instead.'

'Are they really on together?' I try to imagine it and screw up my nose.

'Yeah. Gross, isn't it? They do it in his office, on that green leather couch he's got in there.' Dobie sits on a desk near me and examines her fingernails, which are blue today.

'How do you know? You're making it up.'

'Would I make up something like that? I heard them, panting and groaning, then she walked out with her hair all messed up, shoving her pantyhose in her bag.'

'Sex is so disgusting, the way adults do it.' Oops, I didn't mean to say that. She'll think I'm Miss Prim.

'From what I can tell, they only do it with people they're not married to.'

'If only. My dad should've had a girlfriend. It might've...' There I go again, opening my big mouth, letting out stuff that's totally secret. She's sneaky, getting me to talk like this. No, she's not. I can't blame her. That's me being childish now.

Dobie picks at her thumbnail and little bits of blue paint flick into the air. 'What did you have to go and see Hornsby for? You don't have to tell me if you don't want to, I'm just nosy, that's all.'

I line up all the bits of pen in a nice, neat pattern. 'He wanted to tell me all about the school benevolence fund.'

'What – does he want you to donate some money or something?'

'No. He wanted to *give* me some. Ms Rogers has been bugging him about me being a fucking charity case.' I glare at her. 'Thanks to you.'

'Me? I never said anything to anyone.'

Is she really surprised or is she faking it?
'It was you who hosed me so I had to change
my clothes. Ms Rogers…' I can't say it, can't
even think about it without going berko.

'Hey, I told you I didn't mean to get you.
It was supposed to be Spike coming around
that corner. Truly.' She does look sorry. I
don't think she's putting on an act. I'm not
sure what to say. 'Is that why you copped
detention? Did you do something to Ms
Rogers?'

I shake my head, remembering Hornsby's
face again, how my words seemed to hang in
the air then splatter all over him. In about
two seconds, he went from being all nice
and sympathetic, which was making me
sick anyway, to having a red-nosed hissy
fit. Enough like Dad to freak me right out.
Three days in detention was nothing.

Dobie doesn't get it at all so I explain,
keeping it short. Hornsby's first little
concerned lecture about how I wasn't

settling in to the school, would I like to see the counsellor? Perhaps if my mother wasn't able to help then could he talk to my father..? Which was when I'd lost it and said all those nasty words. She grins when I recite them but doesn't interrupt, so I go on to the second lecture today, the offer of funds, 'A little helping hand...' I was very well-behaved, I didn't curse today; I just stared at him until he gave up.

'I see Ms Rogers looking at you sometimes,' Dobie says. 'I wondered what that was about.'

'I don't need help. I need people to leave us alone.'

All at once, I wish it wasn't true, I wish that I could have friends, a normal family, long sessions on the phone every night. *Fun*, for God's sake. At the very least, a mother who could hold it together better, who could look after *me*. I used to have friends around after school every day. She baked biscuits for us, bought a trampoline for the back yard, watched us swimming while she lay on the banana lounge. She was so normal before Dad came home at night.

'Does your mother laugh? With you, I mean.'

'Er, no way.' Dobie frowns. 'She has this smile she uses a lot. It looks nice but it's not real. It disappears very quickly when no one's around.'

My bones feel heavy but my head's buzzing. I stand and walk up and down the row of desks a couple of times, then I open the door. 'It's like a prison in here. I wish it was five o'clock.'

'Only fifteen minutes to go. Did you do your algebra?'

'I can't. It's driving me nuts.' The book is lying open on the desk but I can't bear to try again.

Dobie walks over and reads my hopeless attempts at the first problem. 'I thought you were good at maths.'

I shrug. 'Usually it's cool. I guess my brain isn't working right now. The harder I try, the more I mess it up.'

'In this one, you've tried to work out *y* first. If you start with *a* and then multiply here...' She bends over the page with the ink tube from inside my pen, trying to write with it.

'How come you know how to do it?' I scrabble around in my bag and find another pen, hand it to her and watch as she neatly writes out the workings of the problem.

'I told you, I fail the tests on purpose. Yeah, I know, dumb thing to do.'

'Mr Canto thinks you *are* really dumb. So do all the other kids. Doesn't that bug you?'

'It didn't at first, but now... yeah, it does, a lot. I hate people thinking I'm stupid.'

I check over the problem she's just finished. 'How did you do that? I still don't get it – sorry.'

'Don't keep saying sorry! Uh... sorry. I didn't mean to be rude.' Dobie smiles at me and the angry words that were on the tip of my tongue slide away. 'Sit down,' she says. 'Let's cruise through these and then we can get out of here.'

I wonder if Mum's home yet. Panic starts to flutter in my stomach and something must show on my face.

'It's only algebra,' Dobie says, laughing, then she waits. The silence is too big to leave empty.

'It's my mum. She, um, I hope she got home from work OK. I...' No, I can't go there, it's too hard to explain. 'I found a kitten this morning, behind a garbage can. I left it in the bathtub.'

'Without water in it, I hope.'

I think of the kitten's big eyes, gazing up at me, and I smile, just a little bit. 'I left it some milk, but it's crawling with fleas. Mum'll freak when she sees it.'

'Is it cute? What colour is it?'

'All black. I thought I could name it Midnight, but Mum won't let me keep it.'

'I know the feeling. None of us have ever been allowed pets.' She taps her pen on the desk. 'Worry about that later. Algebra first. Like forcing down your Brussels sprouts so you can enjoy your French fries.'

I watch and listen as she works through another problem, explaining each step. At first it's like in class, the words spinning around my head but none going in, then I start to see what she's doing, and how she's doing it. It's just like the exercises we did last week, except harder, with more steps. Why couldn't I see that before?

'Now you do the next one,' she says, handing me the pen. I freeze. What on earth is wrong with me? 'What's the first step?' She's much more patient than Mr Canto. He gets irritated if you don't catch on fast, and gives you more exercises to do.

As if that helps, when you don't get it in the first place.

'Um, start with a again?'

'Yep. And then what?'

In three minutes, I have that problem whipped. The answer glares up at me. 'Is it right?'

'Sure is. Do the next one.'

I tackle them one at a time, and each one gets easier. It's like I always knew how to do it, but I'd forgotten for some reason. I want to hug her.

'This is just brilliant. Thank you so much.' I don't think she'll go for a hug so I squeeze her arm instead. She looks kind of surprised and a bit embarrassed.

'Hey, no big deal.'

The door has opened and we didn't even notice. Hornsby stands there, arms folded.

'Gossiping or working?' he says.

'Working,' says Dobie. 'Algebra. Do you want to check?'

'No, er, that's fine.' He clears his throat. 'It's five past five. You can go now.'

We grab our bags and get out of the room as fast as we can. At the school gates, I ask, 'Which way do you go?'

Dobie frowns. 'I catch the 420 bus over there to downtown, then the 17 home.'

'You live miles away! Weren't there bad schools your mother could put you in closer to home?'

She's fidgeting with her jeans, pulling at the seams. 'This school had just been in the newspapers, some survey about learning standards. Actually, I selected it. I thought it would be the one that got up her nose the most. Hey, what am I going to do about these jeans? This is mega-embarrassing.' She turns around and I have to agree – the bit where they've ripped open is showing all her undies. There's no way she can pretend it's deliberately trendy.

'Um, I guess you could come home with me and try to sew them up. I mean, we don't have a sewing machine, just needle and thread.' I know I don't sound very inviting. It's the thought of her seeing our scummy apartment and the lifts with pee in them – if she thinks the school is bad, it's got nothing on where I live.

'I wouldn't know how to use a sewing machine anyway. That'd be great – if you don't mind.'

It's not me who's going to mind. It's Dobie when she sees our place. 'Sure. Don't you have to be home though?'

'Mother won't notice if I'm not there. Even if she does, it'll probably be a relief for her. She can keep making all her plans, which don't include asking my opinion.'

We walk down the street, talking and laughing; the afternoon sun warms my face and it's like we could be two friends walking anywhere, having a good time. 'Plans about what?'

Dobie growls deep in her throat; it startles me for a moment. 'She's manoeuvred me into going back to Barton. That's the pathetic girls' school I got expelled from.'

'Expelled? What did you do?' I can't imagine getting expelled.

She laughs. 'I pretended I was selling drugs to the other girls. Uppers and stuff. I wasn't really. They were those little peppermint candies, but the girls there are so moronic that they believed me, and paid me lots of dollars.'

I want to ask her why she did it. I guess the answer would be *to annoy my mother,* but I don't understand that either. There are lots of things I'm dying to ask her, but that means if she answers, she'll ask me questions too. How can I answer them? Even if I could talk about it all, there's the secrecy thing. Mum and I have only survived this long by not telling anyone who we really are, or why we're running.

It's funny. Dobie's as different from me as she could be, but I used to live like her. Money, clothes, nice house. I was supposed to go to a private school when I got to high school but we left before that. A little light blinks on in my head; I wonder if her mother is like my dad, if she's into controlling people and owning them. Before I can follow this thought, Dobie says, 'Did I shock you?'

'Huh? No, I was thinking...' My brain backtracks. 'If you got expelled for that, how come they're taking you back?'

'Mother bribed them. She's an expert. They couldn't resist.' Dobie kicked at an empty beer can on the sidewalk.

'So... you're leaving the Gate? When?' I should be glad to see the back of her but instead I feel hollow.

'Don't know. She won't say. I think it's part of her strategy, to make me stress out over it. I haven't given up the fight yet, don't worry. She doesn't win that easily.'

We turn into my street and I swallow hard, trying not to see the rubbish, the bare dirt, the broken brick walls, the graffiti. Usually I *don't* see it. I'm used to it. Now I'm looking through Dobie's eyes, and it's pretty ugly.

'You live in this street? That must be hard.' She's chewing on a thumb nail, her head on one side. She sounds a bit astonished, not at all snooty.

'It's what we can afford right now. One day we'll have a house again, maybe when I'm working.' We're in front of my building. I don't give her time to think about the lift, just head up the stairs. She's puffing by the time we reach my floor but she's still gawking around like she's on an archaeological expedition. Maybe I should have let her ride up in the lift after all. Somewhere on the floor below, someone is playing *50 Cent* with the bass up so high that I can barely hear the words above the thumping. I unlock my door and go in without waiting for her.

'Hello, Liss, where have you been?'

That stops me in a hurry. I'd been so worried about Dobie's reaction to where I live that I'd forgotten about Mum! She comes out of our little kitchen and peers over my shoulder at Dobie. The nose and eyebrow rings are not going down very well, neither is the purple spiked hair. 'Hi, Mum. Um, I've been at school…' Can't say in detention, she'll freak.

'…with me. Hello, I'm Dobie.' Dobie holds out her hand and Mum shakes it, smiling. She seems OK so far, not giving Dobie a hard time; she's also not shaky or slurring her words as far as I can tell.

'Hello, Dobie. Liss, you didn't tell me you had a new friend.'

'Er, I haven't.' Because I hate Dobie.

Don't I? 'I mean, we've been in the same class all term but...' I sound hateful and Dobie looks a bit embarrassed. 'We only got to know each other properly this week.'

'Ah. Would you like a coffee and some muffins? I bought double choc chips on the way home.' She opens the brown paper bag and the rich, sweet smell drifts out. My stomach grumbles louder than the music downstairs.

'That'd be great, Mum. First we have to fix Dobie's jeans. I'll go find the sewing box.' I think it's in the hall cupboard; that's where we keep inessential stuff we can leave behind if we have to. As I pull open the door, the music downstairs cuts out and I hear a meow that's no longer squeaky, it's more like a siren.

'What is that noise?' Mum says behind me. 'I thought I heard it when I came home. It's not in here somewhere, is it?'

'Yeah, it is. Sorry. I didn't know what else to do with it.' I figure if I keep talking fast, she'll be OK about it. 'I know I can't keep it, I know that, I haven't even given it a name or anything, but I couldn't leave it to die. Maybe I could take it to the RSPCA.'

'You haven't told me what *it* is yet.'

'Can I see?' says Dobie. 'Is it still in the bath?'

'It's a kitten, a black one.' I hate the tears that smart in my eyes and I blink them back hard. 'I'll take it to the RSPCA tomorrow.' The sooner, the better. That way I definitely can't get attached to it.

Mum opens the bathroom door, an inch at a time. The kitten hasn't managed to scale the sides of the bath so we all squeeze into the tiny room to stare down at it. It stares back and lets out that almighty yowl again, then tries to scrabble out of the bath, making it halfway up before sliding down in a little heap again.

'Hey, he's really cute,' says Dobie, reaching down to pick it up.

'He? It could be a she. Watch out for all its fleas.'

'Fleas?' Now Mum has that edge in her voice that I've been waiting for and I need to sidetrack her somehow, but Dobie beats me to it.

'We'll wash it, right now. The fleas'll be gone in a few minutes. Got some gentle soap and a little brush, Goody?'

'Goody?' Mum's frowning, looking suspiciously from Dobie to the kitten and back again. 'Who's Goody?'

Much as I hate to, I explain. 'It's just a nickname Dobie's got for me, that's all.' Dobie's cuddling my kitten, tickling it under its chin. I want her to give it to me, not to claim it like it's hers, and I want Mum to *go away*, right now. 'Can we have a muffin now, Mum?'

It works. She says, 'Wait until I make coffee,' and turns away at last, heading for the kitchen. Relief floods through me, a warm rush that makes me sag against the doorway. So far, so good.

'Here, he's yours, you hold him while I fill the sink.'

I cradle the tiny, furry thing in my arms and all at once, I love Dobie. How did she know? 'How can you tell if it's a he or a she?'

'I already looked.' She swishes the bar of soap around in the water. 'It's a he, trust me. That's OK, Midnight can be a name for a boy.'

'I told you, Mum won't let me keep it. She's already upset about it.'

'Is she? I didn't notice.' Dobie adds more cold water. 'There, not too hot. Ready?'

'I can tell when she's getting edgy about something. She'll keep fussing until she builds it up into something major. Easier to avoid it if I get rid of it tomorrow.' I try to extract the kitten from my arm but he digs his claws in like he's seen water before and he's terrified. We unhook him from my skin, paw by paw, and I lower him gently into the water. He paddles desperately, trying to get out.

'Hold him by the scruff of the neck, like his mum would,' says Dobie.

When I do as she says, he quietens down and suffers the soap and being wet. Fleas are floating in the water already and Dobie picks more off his fur as she spots them. Wet, he's a scrawny piece of nothing, like a baby rat but still with those huge eyes. When we've got rid of the worst of the crawlies, I grab the old towel we use as a bathmat and wrap him up in it.

'Dry him off a bit,' says Dobie, letting the water out of the sink and making sure all of the fleas are washed down the plughole. 'Then you can brush some more out before he starts licking.'

'How do you know all this?' I can feel the kitten shivering inside the towel.

'My grandma had cats and one of them had two kittens once. I was there when the cat was giving birth. It was awesome.' For a moment, her face lights up with that great smile, then she scowls and turns away. She's like an early spring day, sometimes sunny and bright, and sometimes a storm arises out of nowhere.

CHAPTER 12
Dobie

Why does thinking about Grandma still hurt so much? It's more than three years since she died. Remembering her and me crouched next to the cat in its box, drinking hot chocolate and watching to make sure nothing went wrong because she was an old cat – it's like a big hand has grabbed my guts and twisted hard. Grandma always knew about what was important, how a cat having kittens was about new life, how baking cookies was an art that needed lots of practice so we baked dozens, how dancing was an expression of the soul. That's what she said, anyway, and she said it to Mother as well.

Mother's reply to that was, 'Then ballet is the highest expression, one well worth striving for.' She wouldn't give in. Modern dance was 'common', experimental choreography was prancing around showing off half-nude bodies, and the music was just noise. I'd started off with ballet when I was seven, but by the time I was ten, my passion was modern dance: ballet was boring and restrictive.

Goody sits on the futon couch, cuddling the black kitten, and starts brushing its fur with an old toothbrush, the only thing she could find. I fill the toothbrush cup with water and keep picking up fleas, dunking them in the water until they drown and float. Much simpler than squashing them. I don't know what Goody's on about with her mum. She seems OK to me. A bit paranoid maybe. She's like a saint next to my mother.

There's a clatter in the kitchen and something smashes on the floor. 'Shit.' Goody's face goes all tight and she hands me the kitten, heading for the kitchen. I try not to eavesdrop (that'd have to be a first for me) but this place is so small I can't help it.

'It was just a plate, Lissy. Look, I've cleaned it up.'

'Mum, have you taken two pills again?' Silence. 'You were fine when you came home. Why did you take two?' Goody sounds like she's trying not to cry.

'I just… it's hard, you know. You brought someone, I didn't expect it. She looks like a criminal. All those holes in her face. And the kitten.' Her voice slurs a little. I make it my mission to extract every single flea off this kitten.

'I told you, I'll take it to the RSPCA tomorrow, I promise.'

'But I don't want you to! It's not fair. Why shouldn't you keep it? You have nothing, just your stupid mother who drags you around the country. God, I'm so sick of this!' She's crying but it sounds funny, like she's doing it in slow motion. A chair scrapes across the linoleum.

'Mum, sit down and drink your coffee.

I'll make you some dinner soon. Eat a muffin. It's OK. Don't cry, all right?' There's pouring, clinking spoons, muffled crying still, then Goody emerges carrying two mugs of coffee. 'I'll just fetch the muffins,' she says, putting the mugs down on the side table without looking at me.

'OK.' The kitten is purring. 'Hey, he likes this. I think I've got most of the fleas.'

Goody checks the toothbrush cup. 'Yuck. I'll tip it out.' The crying in the kitchen has died away; she comes back with four muffins on a plate. 'Have one. They're from the bakery down the street. Better than home-made.'

I give the kitten back to Goody and take a muffin, munching slowly; I watch her brushing as I scan the room at the same time. Three of these lounge rooms would fit into our dining room. We've got cupboards bigger than the bathroom. There are no pictures anywhere; the walls are bare, the floors have no rugs, the couch is a futon that someone obviously sleeps on, judging by the pillow on the floor. Probably Goody.

The muffin is brilliant, soft and rich and chocolatey. I could eat about twenty of them, but I leave the rest on the plate for Goody and her mum. Goody puts the kitten on the floor where he shakes himself and tries a few licks before opening his mouth and yowling. Within seconds, there's a bowl of milk in front of him. He laps and purrs at the same time which is so funny that Goody and I get the giggles.

'He sounds like he's purring under-water,' she says. 'Hey, Midnight, slow down.' She strokes the top of his head with one finger. This girl will not be taking this kitten to be put down tomorrow, trust me. I check my watch. It's well after six – should I phone home? Hmmm, what's the best strategy? Am I being good or not? Will it change Mother's mind about Barton? No.

'What about your jeans?' Goody says. 'This furry thing sidetracked me. I'll get the sewing box.' The kitten has finished the milk and its tongue rasps on the bowl.

Goody puts an old chocolate box down in front of me and sits on the floor, picking up

Midnight who immediately starts padding on her stomach. I open the box and check out the rows of coloured thread, the square green pincushion, the scissors and folder of needles. This is so dumb. I don't know where to start. I've never sewn a thing in my life. She'll think I'm totally useless, and I am.

'Do you want to take your jeans off in Mum's bedroom?' Goody thinks I'm shy. Well, that's better than useless.

'No, it's OK.' I jump up and undo the button, pull down my jeans and step out of them. When I hold them up, the rip looks gi-normous. 'Oh, wow, these are history. Are they worth fixing?'

'Not really. But you only need to sew them up enough to get home. Here, hold him.' We swap the jeans and the kitten. Goody picks black thread out of the box, cuts off a length, threads a needle and begins stitching. While I tickle Midnight under the chin, I watch closely. I figure if I ever manage to get away from Mother, I'll need to know this kind of stuff.

I can see it'll take a while. I can't help it, I have to ask. 'Er, is your mum OK?'

'Sure.' Goody hooks through two more stitches. 'Sort of. She's taken two of her tranquillisers, instead of one. They make her really slow and dopey when she does that.' Four more stitches. 'She kind of goes through cycles where she's worse than usual. This is one of them.'

'Is she sick?'

'No.' Goody looks me straight in the eyes as if she's testing me out. 'She's terrified out of her wits. She keeps waiting for Dad to find us again. Next time he might kill her. But not if I have anything to do with it.' She looks down again and keeps stitching.

Her words blast through my mind. Her dad is one of those maniac husbands? They're on the run from him? Does this kind of thing really happen to people outside of TV? It's almost too weird to believe, except she said it and I don't think she'd make up something like that. I hope my face is staying blank. I'd hate to be like one of those people salivating over a gory road accident or murder. I'm so rattled, I don't know what to say next. I honestly don't want to be a snoop, but I can't sit here and say nothing.

'How long have you been, er, on the move?'

'Running. We've been running for two and a half years. This is our third hidey-hole. He's found us twice.' She twists her mouth around and then bites her lips. Her tone is flat, like she's trying to be factual about it, trying to make it sound an everyday thing. But it's not. It's horrible, scary. In fact it's totally fucking terrifying. How can they live like this? Well, they don't, der-brain! They hide, like she said, and her mum has to take tranquillisers to cope.

'That's... this is... God, I'm so sorry.' Goody glares at me and I stumble on. 'I mean, I'm not piling pity on you 'cos I know you'd hate that.'

She shrugs. 'It's OK. When I told you just then, I thought I was going to be sick. It's such a big secret, you know? McCardle's not even my real name. We have to live now with just the essentials, ready to run again. I can't have friends or anything.' She knots the thread and cuts it. 'Or boyfriends. I had one once. Jamie. In the first city we lived in. He was so cool. He played the guitar in a band with his friends. One day I was there, getting ready to go to the movies with him the next night, then the next day I was gone. I couldn't even write and tell him what happened and why in case Dad found out we were friends and interrogated him.'

One tear drips down her face onto my jeans and she brushes at her eyes. 'I'm used to it now. If it's what we have to do, we do it.'

'So me being here is not a good idea. No wonder you tried to brush me off.'

'No, I didn't – well, yeah, I guess I did.' She smoothes my jeans down and folds them neatly. 'I hated you the most, I think, because you had everything that I used to have and you just wanted to chuck it away.'

'I'm not a spoiled bitch, truly.' Goose bumps have blossomed on my legs and I rub them, trying not to shiver. The sun's nearly down and this room has grown chilly. 'There are reasons why I'm fighting my mother, important reasons. They'd probably sound pathetic next to your problems, but they're important to me.' I think about telling her now, but it would sound so feeble after what she's revealed to me that I keep my mouth shut. She doesn't need to hear my whining anyway.

Goody hands me my jeans. 'There you are. That should get you home.'

That's an invitation to leave if ever I heard one. But I can't blame her. She looks pale, her face drawn tight, and she still has to deal with her mum who's probably passed out. 'Thanks a million. I mean, I could've worn my underpants on the outside and pretended I was the new Superwoman but that might've got me arrested.'

I've raised another smile which makes me feel better. I pull on my jeans and button them up. 'If I lost some weight, this wouldn't happen.' Oh boy, now I sound like my mother. I pick up my backpack, ready to go, but I don't want to leave it like this. 'Hey, do you want to – would you be able to – come shopping tomorrow?'

'Where?'

'Not the shopping centre where I live! It's the pits, full of airheads trying to fit into size zero clothes. I mean the big Hillcrest one. No one'll know us there, we can hang out, have coffee, whatever.'

'Can I call you? I don't know, maybe it would be OK.' She grimaces. 'Except I have to take the kitten first.'

'You won't. Midnight's here to stay. Your mum will be fine about him, I just know it.' I scribble my mobile phone number for her on a piece of paper ripped from my notebook. 'Talk to you soon, OK?'

'Sure. Bye.'

Midnight's crawled up to her neck and is cuddling in under her chin. For a moment, I want to stay, to play with the kitten, eat dinner, talk all night, but I can't. I shut the front door behind me and set off down the stairs. Man, it smells like someone's peed on the landing. I speed up, down the last flight, past the lift, across the concrete plaza and up the street to my bus stop. It'll be after eight before I get home. While I'm waiting for the bus, I pull out my mobile and call the phone in the kitchen. Only Nancy answers that one. She's the only person I need to tell.

CHAPTER 13
Melissa

In all this time we've been on the run, Mum and I have never had a fight. Sometimes we've been so scared that we've cried together, sometimes I've been so angry that I wanted to smash everything around me and Mum's calmed me down. She should've been at school the day I screamed at Hornsby.

Now we're fighting, and it's horrible. It's all my fault. In one day I brought two dangerous or stupid things into our safe house. I can't work out what Mum's madder about, Dobie or the kitten. In fact, I can't even work out what she's saying. She's doped up and crying and the words are tumbling out in streams like her tears. I hate to resort to alcohol but it's the only thing that might settle her a bit. I've tried talking, hugging (she pushed me away), holding her hand (same) and yelling. So I pour her a glass of wine and watch her chug it down while I make her a peanut butter sandwich to hold her until dinner is ready.

All the time I'm trying to stay calm, but inside I'm getting angry and it's taking over from the guilt. Why can't she pull herself together for once? I keep thinking about dragons, what Dobie and I talked about. What was that? Crap to make her feel better? Outsmart a dragon by super tactics? Yeah, right. I can't even deal with the person I love most in all the world, the one I have to protect.

I need to do something practical. Mum's bought pork chops that I set to grill before peeling potatoes and finding some peas in the freezer. When I turn around next, Mum is sitting staring into space. She's run out of steam for now, thank God. I sit down opposite her at the tiny table and wait. I'm not going to talk first so I link my fingers together and sit staring at them until she cracks. She can't stand silence between us at any time. She even has to talk to me when I'm in the bathroom.

'Who is that girl?'

I try to judge her tone but it doesn't seem angry, more puzzled. 'She's from my school, Mum, but she doesn't live around here.'

'I can tell. Speaks too nicely. Face like a pincushion though.' She licks her lips and I fetch her a glass of water. She frowns but drinks some of it.

'She's OK. She won't tell anyone... you know.'

'Kitten?'

'I found it by the garbage bins next door. It would've been dead by tonight if I'd left it.' I'm determined not to whine.

'Keep it.'

'Huh? You mean it?' I don't dare to hope yet.

'Yep. It'sh little.' She's slurring a tiny bit but her eyes are OK.

I turn the chops over and sit down again. 'I thought I'd call it Midnight.'

'Good name.' She smiles but it wobbles off her face again. 'Midnight flit. That's what they ushed to call it when you left in the middle of the night to get out of paying rent you owed. That's what we might have to do.' She bows her head and I see tears form on her eyelashes.

Now I understand. 'Have you seen Dad? Mum? Have you?'

'I'm not sure,' she whispers. 'No. I don't think so. But I thought I did. Yesterday. I've been feeling, you know…' She flaps her hand. 'I know it usually doesn't mean anything.'

I wait while she drinks more water, my heart thumping under my ribs. I can't say anything right now.

She takes a deep breath. 'It's because the car is out of action. When we have no car, I feel trapped. I saw someone walk past the display window at the front of the office and stop to look in. He... I thought it was him, just for a second. The sun was behind him. When he kept walking, I could see it wasn't really him at all. It was just some man looking at the display of cards and postcards and stuff. But it gave me a fright. And I've been having those dreams again...'

We sit in silence for a couple of minutes. Is she being paranoid or is it possible it's him? Oh, anything's possible, especially that.

'Mum, how about we eat dinner and you think it all through, then you tell me if you honestly think we've got something to worry about. You always think better when you've eaten properly.'

She smiles, relieved, then gobbles her dinner down like she hasn't eaten in a week. Well, we haven't, not properly. Just toast and soup and eggs. Maybe that's why my brain can't do algebra! I need meat. I force some of the pork chop down my throat, one tiny well-chewed mouthful at a time, saving bits for the kitten. The potatoes and peas stick even worse and I have to wash them down with water, but at last I've managed it. All I have to do now is not throw up. I look at Mum and she nods.

'You're right. The car's made me imagine things. Bobby said he'd have it fixed by tonight so we've got nothing to worry about. Except paying him, of course, but the agency finally gave me what they owed me from that obnoxious florist, so I can give him half tomorrow when he brings it back.' She beams at me. All is right with the world again, at least for now.

Shall I push my luck? 'Um, Dobie wanted to know if I'd go to Hillcrest with her tomorrow. Not shopping, we can't afford that, just to hang out and stuff. She's nice, really, even though she looks...'

'Like the leader of a shoplifting gang.' Mum's eyes are twinkling so I know she's joking. 'I guess you can go, as long as you're careful. Eyes in the back of your head, full alert, all that.'

'It's second nature by now, Mum.' How I wish it wasn't. Even cops freak me out.

'Hmmm... Anyway, who says you can't go shopping? At the very least, you'll have to buy cat food.' Her eyelids are drooping, a signal the pills are taking over again. I help her to bed, undress her and tuck her in, planting a kiss on her forehead before I turn out the light. At least she ate tonight, which means tomorrow she'll wake up fairly normal rather than like a zombie.

While I'm washing the dishes, I smell something incredibly foul. Is there rotten food in the fridge I've forgotten about? Surely not. Then I realise and go searching. Sure enough, there's a neat little pile of

Bone Song

poop on the bathroom floor. Midnight's in the lounge, washing his ears and face. 'OK, kiddo, cat food *and* a litter tray. I get the message.' I'm glad he kept that little errand for after Mum went to bed.

CHAPTER 14
Dobie

All the way home, I can't stop thinking about Goody and her mum. I can't imagine what it's like to live that way, scared all the time, not even able to have a kitten or anything. I always thought Goody was such a suck, doing everything the teachers said, so quiet that she might as well have been part of the furniture. Now I see why. It'd be like being in the Witness Protection programme except there's no one to protect you, there's just you and someone who wants to find you and kill you.

My skin crawls and for a moment I think there's a hand on my shoulder. I spin around in my seat but there's no one. The bus is nearly empty, just me and a drunk old man up near the driver, singing. I wait for my second bus, hiding behind the big bushy plants in concrete tubs that line the street. Why do I feel scared? It's not me who's being hunted. But it's after dark, there are guys cruising in cars and this is not a safe part of downtown.

The bus wheezes in to the stop, the doors open with a whoosh. Twenty minutes and I'll be home; even though Nancy is waiting to scold me for being so late, I don't mind. That's normal, so normal that I can't wait to see her frowning face and hear her giving me what-for.

I sprint up our street, through the side gate and burst into the kitchen, puffing, with a stitch in my side. I'm so unfit. I used to jog, do weight training, the whole thing. Now I'm a blob. I hate that.

'About time, miss.' Nancy glares at me, her arms folded.

'I did call,' I gasp. 'It was important. I

wasn't hanging out anywhere, getting into trouble, I swear.'

'Your mother has asked me four times already where you are.'

'I was at a friend's. Truly, I was.' I remember my jeans. 'Look, I had to go to her house to fix my jeans. They're history, though. I'll have to throw them out.' I turn around so she can inspect my bum.

'How'd you manage that?' She picks at a thread. 'Good sewing job.'

'Um, I jumped off a desk and landed funny. Goody, I mean, Melissa, she sewed it for me.'

'Didn't think *you* did it. What d'you mean, jumped off a desk?' She's got a glimmer in her eyes and I can't help reacting.

'I wasn't dancing! Or anything like that. I was trying to open a window.' All the time I was doing physio, hoping and hoping that I'd be able to dance again, Nancy was the only person who kept me going, dragging me out of bed to do the exercises and buying me dance magazines, anything she could think of. When I called it quits, she still didn't give up. I think she believes dancing might save my soul if I went back to it; might turn me back into the nice person I used to be. It's never going to happen.

'Keep your hair on. I was just wondering.' She jerks her head sideways. 'You'd better go and show your face in there, keep your mother happy.'

'She is last on my list of people to keep happy.' But I go anyway. Mother is watching television and flicking through a pile of the latest fashion and décor magazines. She glances up, tries to pretend she hasn't been waiting for me.

'Where have you been? It's nearly nine.'

'At a friend's house.'

'Who? Jeannie? Or Anna? I thought you didn't see them these days.' She stares down at a picture of a super-skinny model wearing a simple black sheath.

'Melissa. She's from my school.' I wait for the inquisition.

'Well, when you go back to Barton, you won't be able to see her any more.'

'Why not? Besides, I told you, I'm not going back to Barton.' Why is she being such a bitch? I don't understand. What difference does it make to her what I do? Or is this just about winning? Maybe it is. I guess that's what it's been about for me, up till now.

'Then you'll have to go to boarding school.' That little cat smile appears and I want to hit her.

'OK.' I shrug. 'If I go to boarding school, we won't have to look at each other or talk to each other. I'm sure that'll make you very happy.'

That's got her. She didn't expect me to choose boarding school. It was her last resort.

That choc chip muffin was really delicious. I realise I'm starving and head back to the kitchen. Nancy points towards the fridge and I find a covered plate of food that I programme the microwave to reheat. While I wait, my mind zings back to Goody again. I lean against the bench where Nancy is beating up pancake mix for tomorrow's breakfast.

'Nancy, have you ever known someone whose husband tried to kill them when they left?'

She gives me a sharp look and beats harder. 'Why're you asking a question like that?'

'I, um, I heard a kid at school talking about it today. And don't do the Mother thing about what a terrible school it is and I shouldn't be associating with people like that.'

'Sounds to me like you're finding out about the real world. Not that wife-beating is just for poor people. Plenty of rich men do it too.' She lets the batter sit for a moment to see if air bubbles rise, then gives it a few more stirs. 'Sometimes the more a man has, the more he thinks his wife is just another thing to own. Then again, poor men with nothing much think they own their wives too. Men just like to own things, I guess.' She covers the bowl and puts it in the fridge.

'But why can't someone leave if they want to? I don't get it. It's crazy.'

'Yep, crazy's the word.'

The microwave beeps and I fetch my plate, sit down and start eating. It's a red night tonight, chicken with red peppers, spicy beetroot and carrots.

'I've finished down here. You put your plate in the dishwasher and press the button, all right?' She waits for me to nod. 'And you watch yourself with your friend. If her dad's crazy, you don't want to get in the way. You can help best by staying out of it.'

I open my mouth to deny it's anything to do with me, but she's gone. She means well but I can't stay out of it. Ignoring what's happening to Goody and her mum would be like... like pretending Mother is a loving, caring parent. Huh!

In my bedroom I pull out my guitar and play a bit to loosen my fingers up, then I get my notebook and try out the new song I've written. I still can't get the lyrics but the melody is all there. I play it over and over, experimenting and changing little bits until I'm satisfied, then I copy it out neatly again in my old music book from Barton. I must buy a new one. And a new pair of jeans. That reminds me about going shopping with Goody tomorrow. I hope she can come. I really do.

Funny how two days ago I thought she was the biggest loser ever. Now I quite like her. I wonder if she likes me? I've got so used to everyone hating me, or treating me like a big pain in the bum, that this all feels a bit strange. I hope she does like me.

CHAPTER 15
Melissa

Mum is already up when I wake up even though it's early. Midnight is curled up on the end of my bed in a black ball. The sun angles through the tear in the window blind and creates a streak of light across the green and brown carpet and up the wall. It reminds me of a picture I saw of a hidden lake in the mountains. A few lines of a new poem drift into my head.

'Lissy, you want croissants? They're hot.'

Huh? Since when do we have croissants for breakfast? I slide out of bed, trying not to wake the kitten, and stagger into the kitchen, rubbing my eyes. Mum is fixing coffee so I race back and scribble down what I remember in my notebook.

'Another poem?' Mum's smiling down at me, coffee pot in her hand. 'One day you'll have to start sending them out to get published.'

'I doubt it! They're not good enough for that. They're just a hobby.' *That keeps me sane sometimes.* I follow her back and sure enough, there's a plate of croissants on the table, along with strawberry jam in a little glass bowl. 'Is it your birthday? Did we win the lottery?'

'No. I just thought we deserved a treat today.' She pours coffee into our mugs. 'Bobby is bringing the car over soon. I saw Mrs Hawkins when I went out to the bakery for these.'

'You went to the bakery?' She hardly ever goes out except to work or to do the laundry downstairs. If the machines are broken, I'm the one who has to lug our dirty clothes to the Sudsalot two blocks away.

'Sure. And I haven't had any pills today either.' Her face flushes when she says this and she doesn't look at me.

I'm not sure what to say but I feel like I should say something. 'That's great, Mum.' How long will it last? Lunchtime? What's going on? Why is she suddenly all full of smiles? Why is she being brave? Maybe she's just like me – sick of being paranoid and bad-tempered.

'When you call your friend about going to the shopping centre, tell her I'll drive you both. I can pick her up at her house, all right?' She crunches into her croissant and flakes of pastry fly across the table. Midnight scampers in and looks up at the table hopefully.

I pull two bits off my croissant, feed one to Midnight and chew the other carefully. 'OK, but... she lives across the other side of town, in Brightwood. She has to catch two buses to get home.'

'Oh. I just assumed she lived around

here. Brightwood. That's an expensive part of town. I thought she went to your school.'

'She does. She wants to. I mean, she could go to a private school but... she just doesn't want to, that's all.'

'I guess I could drive to Brightwood, as long as you navigate.'

'You don't have to, Mum, we can catch buses and meet up at Hillcrest. We'll be fine.' Please, Mum, just let me do something normal for a change.

'No, it'll be good for me to get out and drive around a bit. I'll test the car out, make sure it's running OK. You get Dobie's address when you ring and make a time.' She looks so happy that I don't have the heart to say no. I decide to enjoy my croissant and try not to worry about it. Mum frowns when I feed Midnight another piece so I get up and pour some milk into a bowl for him. I sit down and take a bite of my breakfast.

'Is Dobie her real name?'

'No, it's Deborah, but she hates that.' Mmm, warm, flaky, sweet croissant. Yummy. Stop asking questions, Mum.

We drink our coffee in silence and I relax a little. By the time we clean up, I turn my bed back into a couch and Mum's handwashed her blouses for work and hung them over the bath, I'm worried about calling Dobie. What if she's changed her mind? It's not even ten o'clock, she's probably still asleep. I jump when someone knocks at the door, but it's only Bobby with Mum's car keys in his hand.

'It was the water pump,' he says. 'I found you one in a wrecker's yard so it didn't cost as much as I thought.'

'That's wonderful,' says Mum. 'I don't know how to thank you.'

'No problem.' He looks embarrassed and grins. 'You want to come see what I did? I got you a better tyre for that back right too. And I tightened the handbrake.'

'You're amazing,' Mum says. 'All I have to do now is wash it.'

'Oh, I did that too. She's all shined up.'

What is this? Good Neighbour Week? I watch Bobby as he stands back and allows Mum through the door first and it hits me between the eyes. God! Bobby's hot for Mum! I know Bobby's divorced and Mrs Hawkins is pleased about it because she didn't like his wife. Mum's not divorced though. You'd think another man would be the last thing she'd want. But she was in the bar the other night with that guy from work. That's what I hate about the pills. They turn her into someone I don't know, someone I don't want to know.

I turn on the mobile, take a deep breath and call Dobie.

CHAPTER 16
Dobie

I couldn't get to sleep for ages last night. Goody's words kept spinning around in my brain, and I kept trying to imagine what it's been like for them. Stupid, really. I can only go by movies I've seen or stuff on TV – how real is that?

This morning I feel so grumpy and tired that I don't want to get out of bed. I want to pull the covers over my head and stay here for the whole day. Then I remember that I asked Goody to go to Hillcrest with me so I drag myself into the shower and turn the water on hot then cold a few times until I feel reasonably alert.

Since my favourite jeans are wrecked, I have to wear another pair that are too short in the legs for me. I guess I've grown a bit, although it's more out than up. As soon as we get to the mall, I'll have to buy a new pair and put them on straight away. The purple dye in my hair has almost washed out. I gaze at the jar of gel for a long time before I leave it unopened and brush my hair back off my face. In the mirror, I look almost normal apart from the rings and studs. *Normal.* I reach for the gel and scoop out a gob but I don't put it on my hair. I keep staring in the mirror but the person in there is no help at all, so I wash the gel down the sink and head downstairs for breakfast.

I slurp coffee, wolf down blueberry pancakes and wonder when Goody's going to call. I can't call her. For sure, they'll have an unlisted number. I check my phone is fully charged and working.

'Your mother's going to be down in a minute. She says she's taking you shopping.' Nancy folds the dishcloth into a tiny, fat square.

I feel a sharp pain in my stomach and rub the spot. It's not indigestion. 'We've been through this before. I buy my own clothes. Too bad if she hates black.'

'She's not buying those kinds of clothes.'

I know Nancy will always be on my side, but sometimes Mother puts her in a position where she has to be a tattletale and she hates it. I hate it too. I don't see why Mother always has to be manipulating people.

Speak of the devil.

'Deborah, we're going shopping this morning. Are you ready?' Mother stands in the doorway, dressed in yellow. Even her earrings are yellow.

'Shopping for what?' I try to keep calm but I feel like I'm being forced backwards into a dark corner.

'New uniforms for Barton. Since you burned all your old ones, we'll have to completely outfit you again.' She smiles her iron lady smile that says 'Don't you dare argue with me,' but she doesn't know that things have changed for me. I'm not even sure *how* they've changed; all I know is that it's got something to do with Goody and her mum.

I keep my tone as careful and polite and determined as possible. 'Mother, I am not going back to Barton. I told you last night that boarding school would be preferable.'

'Don't be silly. Barton is the best school in the state.' Her lips have thinned until she's almost got no mouth at all.

'I am not going shopping for Barton uniforms.' I stare her out, willing her to drop her eyes and give in but I should know better.

'Fine,' she says. 'You are grounded for the day then. I shall buy them for you and if they are the wrong size, that will be your misfortune. Nancy, please make sure that Deborah does not leave the house.'

How dare she make Nancy responsible? If I go out, she'll take it out on Nancy, and the way Mother is at the moment, she could even fire her. God, I hate her!

While I'm sitting at the table planning my mother's gruesome death, the sound of her car driving away drifts in through the open window. Maybe she'll have an accident and I won't have to do anything.

'I'm nobody's gaoler,' Nancy grumbles. 'That woman asks too much.'

What am I going to tell Goody? Maybe she doesn't want to go with me anyway.

'When my friend calls, I guess I have to tell her I can't go to the mall. Am I allowed to receive one phone call?'

Nancy grins at me. 'Only one from your lawyer.'

I go back upstairs, check my phone again and pace up and down. When the stupid phone trills, I grab it so fast I drop it. When

I finally answer, Goody sounds nervous.

'Er, hi. Um, do you still want to go to Hillcrest?'

'Yeah, of course,' I say. 'I just... er, don't you?' I knew it. She doesn't really want to go, she's trying to find a way to say no. 'It's OK, you don't have to, I know you're worried about going out and stuff...' Then I remember that I can't go anyway so what am I talking about?

'It's not that. It's Mum.' She breathes into the phone. 'She wants to take us. In our car. It's just been fixed and... she says she'll come and pick you up.' Another pause. 'It's a pretty old car.'

Oh. Goody thinks I won't want to go now because I don't want to be seen in an old bomb. I look around my expensively-decorated bedroom, at my thick carpet and velvet curtains. 'No, tell your mum that's great. I'd love to be picked up. I get really sick of catching buses everywhere.'

'I'm sorry, it's not that she's trying to spy on us or anything.'

'Course not. Listen, I'll give you my address and directions. I'll wait down the end of my street, if you like.' Too late, I realise that sounds like I don't want to be seen getting into her car, but it's easier than trying to explain why I'm grounded and have to sneak out. I give her the details, we agree on a time and I hang up.

I trudge downstairs. I'm going to get Nancy into a heap of trouble and she's not going to be happy.

She's putting a load of laundry into the washer. 'You got any clothes you haven't put down the chute?' she asks.

'No, I'm fine.' I lean against the dryer, fiddling with the stud in my nose.

'Leave that alone before you get germs in it.' She inspects the rings and studs, one by one. 'Darned ugly, these are. Sure get a good rise out of your mother though.'

I try to smile. 'I think I'm about to do something that will shoot her off a mountain.'

'Don't tell me, you're planning to go out.'

'I have to.' I explain to her about Goody and the car thing. 'I couldn't say no. She would've thought I was being snobby.'

'This your friend with the crazy father?'

'No, I told you; that was just someone I heard talking.' I look at her with my most truthful face.

'Hmph. You just remember what I said. You watch your back *and* your front.' She pushes buttons on the washer and heads back to the kitchen. 'You still climb out your window?'

'I haven't done that for ages. Haven't needed to.' I used to sneak out to extra dance lessons – Mother allowed me to attend one class a week, on sufferance, but it wasn't enough. Grandma paid for the extra classes.

'If you go sulk in your room and lock the door, how am I supposed to know if you're still in there? Specially if you don't answer the door.' She winks. 'Now I got to vacuum so you better get out of my way.'

I give her a big hug and she laughs. In my room, I lock the door and put the bolt on that I screwed into the frame last year when I discovered Mother had a key. I pull off my black T-shirt and find the plain white shirt that I wore the other night. I'm not taking my jewellery off but the shirt might make Goody's mum a bit happier.

When I open my window, the ground seems a long way away. There's a sloping roof down to where the oak tree branches grow across the guttering. The biggest branch held me OK when I was twelve but I've grown a bit since then. I've changed my boots for trainers so the roof isn't too bad, but half-way down I move a little too fast and slip. I try to grab on to the tiles but no luck, I slide all the way to the gutter, picking up too much speed. Just as well my legs are stuck out in front of me. I jam my feet into the gutter and it rips away from the wall. Shit! For one moment I'm about to career off the roof and down to break every bone on Mother's rock garden, then the gutter holds. My heart bangs up against my ribs like a battering ram.

I've never been a chicken but it takes me several minutes to psyche myself up to reach out for the oak branch and then let my weight rest on it as I inch across. What if I fall? What if I bust something in my shoulder again? The thought of being in hospital totally freaks me out. I push away the images that spring up. *I will not go there again! I would rather die.*

Then it strikes me that if I fall, I probably will die, thanks to all these brown, craggy rocks, huge cacti and other thorny things. Suits Mother though.

I giggle and wobble at the same time and fear gallops through me, making me clutch at the branch in a panic. *Take it easy!* The branch bends a little but it holds me as I creep off the roof and onto it, then along until I reach the trunk. From there, it's easy. The notches I sawed out are still deep enough to get a good grip. I jump down the last three feet and my legs give way. I must've been even more terrified than I thought.

Better get down the street before they leave without me. I jog along the sidewalk, keeping an eye out in case my mother arrives home early, and lean against the big tree on the corner, ready to hide behind it. Not that it'll work. My mother could spot me in a blizzard.

I hear Goody's car before I see it. Cars around here sound different, I guess, smoother and quieter. Goody's car isn't a roaring V8, but it's a bit noisy and her mum grinds the gears as she comes up the rise. Their car is dark green, low to the ground, with rust along the bottoms of the doors. I wave at Goody and step onto the kerb, ready to jump in and get out of here.

Goody's mum stops with a little jerk. When I open the rear door, she says brightly, 'Where's your mum? I was going to say hello.'

Goody's shoulders hunch up. I say, 'She's out shopping. She's really busy today.'

'Oh. Never mind, another time.'

Yeah, right. Then I feel awful. It's not her fault that I live with a dragon. 'Do you know the way to Hillcrest from here? I can direct you the quick way, if you like.'

'All right, that would be great.' Goody's mum taps her fingers on the steering wheel like she's got a tune playing in her head and it makes me smile. 'Melissa is buying cat food today. We've decided to keep Midnight.'

'Hey, that's great!' I tap Goody on the shoulder. 'Are all the fleas gone?' Oops, maybe I shouldn't have mentioned that, although her mum seems OK.

'Yep, I think so. We left him asleep. He tired himself out chasing a ball of paper.' She turns and grins at me. 'I found one tiny, weeny patch of white on him, on his tummy. It's only about the size of a match head.'

'So are you going to change his name to Spot?'

'Nah, Midnight has stuck. I have to buy him a litter box too. He pooped in the bathroom.'

'Lissy! You never told me that.' Goody's mum frowns.

'It's OK, I cleaned it up. He couldn't help it.'

'At least he didn't go on the carpet.' I'm trying to help out here, make that frown go away. I get the feeling that this is the kind of thing Goody does all the time.

I concentrate on giving Goody's mum instructions on where to turn at what street and we're at Hillcrest in a few minutes. She lets us out by the main entrance. 'I'll pick you up at three,' she says.

'Mum, we can catch the bus home!' Goody's face is bright red.

I think about how if her mum takes me home, I might just make it back to my room before my mother guesses what I've done. 'It's OK, we'll be here at three,' I say, and pull Goody inside before she can argue.

'God, I hate that,' Goody says. 'I just wanted a normal day with my friend, shopping and hanging out.'

'I know, but ...' I tell her what's happened and how I'm supposed to be in my room.

'She grounded you for not going shopping? That's a bit weird.'

'The shopping is really about me going back to Barton. I'm refusing to go.' We start walking through the centre, checking out the shop windows. I point towards a jeans shop. 'I need new jeans. Let's try there first.'

'You want to stay at the Gate? That's totally weird. Who would want to stay in the same school as Spike Donivan?'

I screw up my nose. 'You don't know what Barton's like. It's worse than being in the army. They march everywhere in pairs, and the uniform is gross. Like a nun's habit. Anyway, as long as Mother wants me to go there, I'll refuse. I even said I'd prefer to go to boarding school.'

'Would you?' Goody's gazing in the window of the jeans shop at a pair of cream jeans. 'Aren't they gorgeous?'

'They'd look great on you. Why don't you buy them?'

'They're fifty dollars. I can't afford that. My shopping is done at the Salvos.'

I grab her hand and drag her inside. 'Come on, you can try them on at least. While you help me pick some new black ones.'

I find a pair of cream jeans in her size and when I turn around, she's holding a pair of chocolate brown ones. 'Here, you try these for a change,' she says. 'I'm sick of seeing you in black.'

'Yes, ma'am!' We head for the changing rooms, giggling. Goody doesn't know it yet but I'm going to buy her the cream jeans. I've barely touched my pocket money for months and I've got about four hundred dollars in the bank. It's going to be a great afternoon, we're going to have *fun*.

CHAPTER 17
Melissa

I tried to persuade Dobie to buy the chocolate jeans but she wouldn't. So we compromised. She bought blue ones, and then she insisted on buying me the cream ones. I felt awful, like she was just sorry for me having crap clothes, but she said it was a punishment for not letting her buy black again.

Even though we're having a great time, I can't help checking out the crowd all the time. I thought I was doing it sneakily but Dobie soon notices.

'You're always looking for him, aren't you?' she says.

'I guess. It's a habit. I don't think I'll ever feel safe again.' I shiver and clutch my new jeans in their bright red bag.

She opens her mouth to say something but instead she pulls me inside the shop we're walking past. I nearly scream but she's laughing, holding one finger up to her mouth. My heart skitters and I glance around. We're surrounded by multi-coloured glassware and shiny knives, forks and spoons spread out in fans. 'You want to buy some cutlery now?' I ask.

'No, I'm avoiding *them*.' She points outside.

I peer out, feeling the back of my neck tighten. Who is she talking about? Police? Then I see them. 'Oh. Spike Donivan and his gang. What are they doing here?'

'Probably shoplifting.'

There's four of them, all dressed in homie clothes that look totally stupid on them. We wander around the shop, wasting time choosing a table setting each while we wait to make sure Spike has gone.

'Let's go to the supermarket and buy cat food,' Dobie says. 'No way will they be in there.'

The supermarket is frantic, crying kids everywhere and mothers shoving their trolleys around like they want to kill someone. We find some cat food with pretty kitty pictures on the cans, then I pick out a yellow litter tray and a bag of recycled litter.

'What about kitty treats?' Dobie says, pointing to some boxes higher up. 'I'll buy those, my contribution.' She reaches up quickly; a second later she's hunched over, holding her right arm and shoulder, her face twisted in pain.

'What's wrong?' I drop my cans and tray. 'Did something fall on you? Dobie?'

'I'm – fine.' She forces the words out. 'Just give – me a – minute.'

I stand next to her, wanting to touch her, rub her arm, smooth her hair, anything, but I can't because she seems in so much pain. I don't know what's wrong. People push past, staring for a few seconds then moving on with stony faces. Probably think we're druggies or something. I hate that. Finally Dobie straightens up but her face is almost dead white.

'Sorry.' She takes a deep breath. 'Sometimes I forget I can't do that any more. Lift my arm straight up like that. Just won't go.'

'Are you OK? Shall I buy some painkillers for you?' I don't know what else to suggest.

'No, it's fine. It'll go away soon. I just upset it a bit. Can you carry everything?'

'Sure.'

'Let's go and have a coffee then.'

Sounds good to me. I pay at the checkout and we head for the nearest café which is up a level. We're halfway up the escalator when I hear a voice from above.

'Oooh, the two bad girls are out shopping!'

My fingers grip the escalator rail. This is all I need. Just when we were having a great day. Spike Donivan. He leers down at us.

'Whatcha been buying, ladies? Witches' potions? Or love spells? Only way you'll ever get a guy.' His stupid friends laugh and slap each other's hands.

Within a few metres, they've surrounded us. My legs start to tremble and I try to stiffen them, stand tall.

'Aren't you going to talk to us?' Spike demands. 'Not very friendly of you, is it, boys?'

'Nah, real stuck-up, they are,' one of the others says.

'Get out of our way, scuzzball,' Dobie says.

'You shouldn't talk to me like that,' Spike says, moving closer to her. Then he wags his finger in front of her nose. 'You've got a big mouth.'

There's a pounding in my chest that I thought was fear; now I feel something hot in there, something bubbling up. I move next to Dobie, shoulder to shoulder. 'Why don't you piss off, Spike? Before you're sorry.'

'Who asked you?' He looks at me like I'm nothing.

'You did when you got in our way.' The rage has boiled up and I can hear my voice, coming out like a snake's hiss. 'Move aside – *now*.' I stare straight at him, daring him to diss me again. Inside my head, another little panicky voice is saying *What are you doing, you idiot? He'll cream you!*

He's not sure what to do. His friends wait for him to put me down. I want to step forward and punch him right on his porky nose.

'You're blocking the escalator, boys and girls. Take it somewhere else.' A security guard appears at Spike's elbow and he jumps.

His face flushes.

'Yeah, right,' he says. 'You'll keep.' He points his finger again but Dobie and I just stick our noses in the air, turn and head away from them, fast.

'Here – coffee – this'll do.' Dobie takes my hand and guides me into the café. She finds us a table and sits me down. Just as well, my legs were about to give way. She orders and sits down opposite me.

'God, you were awesome,' she says, her eyes shining. 'I thought you were going to plant one right in his ribs!'

'I thought I was too.' I laugh shakily. 'I must've been crazy.'

'He deserved it. He didn't expect it to come from you though. Quiet, mousey Melissa. He nearly died of shock!' She giggles and I do too, then my breath catches in my throat.

'I don't know what gets into me. That's what happened when I yelled at Hornsby. It's like I lose it altogether, go berserk. Scary.' I grip my hands together and take a few deep breaths.

'Just as well that guard turned up. If Spike had decided to call your bluff, I couldn't have helped much.' Dobie rubs her arm again.

Was it a bluff? I don't want to think about that. 'Is it better now? What's wrong with it?'

'It's an old injury, you know, from the war.' She tries to laugh it off but it isn't working. The waitress arrives with our coffees. 'Drink these first and then I'll tell you.' She huddles over her cup, the steam floating up around her face as she stirs in some sugar. She looks so sad that I want to tell her it's OK, she doesn't need to explain, but my curiosity is too strong. I want to know, more than I want to spare her, and that makes me feel mean.

CHAPTER 18
Dobie

The moment has come that I've managed to avoid very successfully for nearly six months. So successfully that I'd even kidded myself that 'The Accident' hadn't really happened. That I'd always been Dobie, the girl with an attitude, the troublemaker, the one with the horrible mother who deliberately made her life a misery.

Who was I kidding? All I'd done was reach for kitty treats and it'd all come crashing back in on me. Now I have a girl with kind eyes who wants to give me a big hug, I know, and she's waiting to hear my sorry story.

'I was a dancer.' Was. That's a good place to start. 'I won every competition I entered, right up to state level. I was training for the nationals, my teacher had worked out this piece, choreographed it to my favourite music, *Clare de Lune*.' Goody knows it, which surprises me. 'I'd worked on it for weeks, practising every night, doing extra classes. My teacher's aunt made my costume, all purple and silver, because my mother refused to have anything to do with it all.' Bitterness is creeping in and I force it back. 'There were going to be people at the nationals, people who were talent scouting, looking for young dancers they could train on scholarships. I could've gone to Chicago or New York, maybe, attended school there while I was dancing. It would've been a dream come true.' This is as far as I can go for a minute or two. I take a swallow of coffee and then stir it again, scraping the sides of the cup.

'It didn't happen, huh?' Goody's voice is soft. I blink hard.

'My mother had a regime we all had to follow. My two older sisters had performed to perfection, followed every rule, done everything her way. Gone to school at Barton, had ballet lessons, not 'tawdry modern dance' like me, learned a suitable musical instrument and had weekly riding lessons. The only way she would allow me to keep going to modern dance was if I obeyed every other command.

'I hated the riding instructor. He expected you to love horses like he did, to think that riding was the best thing in the world. He yelled at me all the time, said I had a seat like a pregnant pig. When I told Mother I wasn't going to go any more, she said if I stopped riding, I had to stop dancing.'

'Didn't she realise how important it was to you?'

'That didn't matter. It wasn't important to her. I didn't tell her about the dance companies and their scouts, but someone must have. She held it over me... so I had to keep riding.'

Goody waits quietly. I'm glad she's not asking lots of stupid questions.

'One Saturday my usual horse wasn't there. It was away or something, so I was told to ride this black thing called Robust. It was a dumb horse, wouldn't do anything it was told without a whip. I hated the whip but I had to use it. We were practising jumps. I'd never been able to jump very well on my old horse, and this one was hopeless. I kept sliding half-off and looking like an idiot. The teacher yelled at me for not using the whip and made me go around again.

'The horse clipped a rail and landed funny. I went forward over its head and the whip caught the horse in the eye. When I hit the ground, that was when my arm broke. That was bad enough, but that horse... that bloody-minded, shitty horse...' I breathe deep, grind my teeth, force the words to keep coming. 'It came back and stomped on me, on my broken arm and shoulder, like it knew where to get me the worst.'

'God, you must've been terrified!'

'I didn't really know what was happening. The pain just took over. Then they carried me off to hospital.'

Images spear through my head. The trolley speeding along the corridor, the overhead lights flashing past like milestones on the way to Hell. The tubes, needles, the smells of acid, disinfectant, fresh blood. The stiff sheets locking me into the bed. The pain. The doctors and nurses who lied and lied, day after day, telling me I would be fine. The specialists who lied, telling me the same. The one who finally told me the truth so matter-of-factly that I wanted to kill him. And after all that, my mother patting me on the head, saying, *Perhaps it's for the best.* Meaning *I've won.*

'She said what?'

I jump. I realise I said the last bit aloud. 'That's what Mother said, after I'd done the physio for months, killing myself with the pain, refusing the painkillers because they made me like a zombie. When I'd finally bitten the bullet and given up hoping. *Perhaps it's for the best.'*

'No wonder you hate her.' Goody nods. 'That's one dragon. Your mother. And your second one is..?'

I try to shrug the question off. Now I've told her all this stuff, I feel pathetic. 'I don't know. I guess...' She waits patiently. She should be a shrink. 'Me. I can't move on from it. I should grow up, get over it. Instead I'm training to be a juvenile delinquent, bent on revenge.'

'Hey, it might not be the best thing for you to do, but at least you're doing something. I mean, you could be hiding in a corner, still hooked on morphine or snorting coke, feeling like shit.' She grins. 'You probably do feel like shit. Sorry. But you know what I mean. You're tough, you're strong. That's a good thing.'

'Hmm, I suppose.' I think of her mum on tranquillisers and decide not to say any more. I've said quite enough already. I check my watch. 'It's nearly three. We'd better head for our pick-up point. Don't want to keep your mum waiting.'

Goody grimaces. 'Yeah, I hope she finds her way back here OK.'

'She will.'

CHAPTER 19
Melissa

Dobie sounds so reassuring when Mum isn't waiting at the entrance for us, that I don't worry too much. We sit on a bench in the sun and talk for a while, but when I check my watch again and it's nearly 3.15, that familiar worm of worry starts to twist itself into knots in my stomach. I stand, walk up and down a couple of times but I can't see our car anywhere. I'm hoping she's arrived early and gone into the mall to look at the shops. Then I start checking for Dad's car. I have no idea what he might be driving. I look for something expensive, shiny and big.

'Do you think maybe she is lost?' Dobie asks. 'I shouldn't have directed her. It's better if you find your own way to a place.'

'It's not that. I've just got… I don't know, it's not like her, that's all. We usually have this thing about being on time. We always have to know where the other one is.' Except if she's taken two pills again, she might be flaked out at home. Damn her! She knows how important it is, and that I'll worry.

She joins me on the kerb and scans the cars around us. 'What will you do if she doesn't turn up soon?'

'Call her first. Just to check.' Not that she'll answer her mobile if she's passed out.

'Here, use mine.' Dobie hands me her phone, already turned on. 'Go on.'

I press in the numbers and listen to it ring. No reply.

'That must mean she's on her way,' Dobie says. 'She's just late.'

Or passed out, I nearly say, but I get a feeling like an icy finger suddenly running down my spine. I spin around and scan the crowd by the doors.

'Something's wrong, I know it.' I want to jump up on the tub nearby that's full of bright orange marigolds, scan the parking lot from end to end, but if Dad's around somewhere, he'll see me. I can't afford to be obvious, this of all times.

Dobie stares at me, then she says, 'You stay out of the way while I look.' And I know she really does understand and wants to help. My eyes burn and I blink hard.

'OK.'

She climbs up on the tub, ignoring grown-ups who glare at her, and hunts slowly from left to right. 'Nothing.'

'Any big, expensive cars cruising around?'

'Nup. None that stand out anyway.' She climbs down again and stands, hands on hips, frowning. 'I guess we just have to keep waiting. Do you have, like, an escape plan?'

'It's simple. We get in the car and drive. That's what we've done the last two times. There's no point making detailed plans because we never know when we might have to leave. Both times so far Mum has been at work. She's had to walk out without even collecting any wages that're owed to her.'

'Wow, that's pretty drastic.' Dobie shakes her head like it's too hard for her to imagine.

I guess it might be. It hits me like a slap in the face – *this is a really stupid, bizarre way to live a life.* No wonder Mum and I are both freaking out all the time. Normal people don't hide like criminals, they don't live like tramps, they don't push away anyone who wants to be a friend.

Then I remember that little gap in the door, the whimpering noise Mum was making, the picture I've never been able to get out of my head of Dad running his knife across her skin and the blood leaping up behind the blade in a long, wet, red line. I have to grip my elbows with my hands as tight as I can and force the picture away.

'Melissa? Are you OK? You're shaking. Here, sit down.' Dobie leads me to the bench and we sit.

I have to tell her she has to go, right now. 'Leave me here. You go. Catch a bus home. You have to.'

'Why? I'm not leaving you. Your mum will be here in a minute.'

'*He* might be here instead.'

'Your dad? We'll run inside, get help.'

'No. It doesn't work that way. He doesn't work that way. If he's got her...' I try to breathe. I feel like I'm choking. 'He has a knife. And a gun. He's said lots of times that he'll use them, either or both. He doesn't care. If he's got her, he'll come here and make me get in the car. You have to go home. You won't be safe either.'

Now she is looking at me like I've got a screw loose. 'How can he do that here? Where everyone could see?'

'You have to go!' I shout.

'No. You're worrying for nothing, because she's late. I'm staying.'

I want to scream at her, hit her, make her go away, but all the time a little voice inside me is squeaking, s*he might be right, you might be carrying on for nothing, you've made these mistakes before, getting all upset for nothing.* I can't let that voice win. In my guts, I know I'm right. *I know I'm right.*

But I do want her to stay. I'm so tired of fighting on my own, looking after Mum, being the brave one, the one who takes charge. If we do have to run though, Dobie's got to stay behind. That's all there is to it.

I hunch down on the bench, my face in my hands. I want it all to go away. I want to be high up on a mountain, with no other people for miles and miles.

'Hey, here's your mum. See, I told you, she just got –'

Brakes screech, Mum screams, 'Melissa, get in the car! Hurry!' and I know I was right all along. I stagger to my feet, try to walk but it's like my shoes are full of concrete. I can hardly move. Dobie grabs my arm and drags me to the car. We fall onto the back seat, her shoving me over, slamming the door behind her. Mum lets out the clutch too fast and the car jerks a few times before it takes off.

'Slow down, Mrs McCardle, it's OK. Take it easy.' Dobie's staying calm, leaning forward over the front seat, talking to Mum, directing her. I slump in the corner. 'Is he following you? Can you see him?'

'No, I don't think so. I think I got away, oh God, I hope he didn't see me!'

Mum's half-sobbing and the car veers across the road.

'What kind of car is he driving?'

'A black Mercedes, I think, or a Lexus; no, a Mercedes. Tinted windows.' Mum glances in the mirror, looks wildly over her shoulder, the car swerves again.

'You drive and I'll keep a look out,' Dobie says. 'Take the next left and head down past the lake, OK?'

'OK.' Mum seems to be calming down a bit, thanks to Dobie. I sit up a bit straighter. I know I should be asking Mum questions, sorting out what's happened, whether she really did see him or not. She's made this mistake before, but she sounds certain this time. I stare out the side window and stay silent.

After a few more minutes, Mum and Dobie decide that we're not being followed. Past the lake, Dobie directs Mum to drive into a large cemetery. 'It's quiet in here, and no one will expect you to be in a place like this.'

Mum pulls the car up next to a huge statue of a weeping angel and rests her head on the steering wheel, crying quietly. Dobie looks at me.

'Now what?' she says.

I shrug. 'We'll have to drop you home, I guess, and then keep going. Head south, maybe, we haven't been that way yet. Or backtrack. I don't know what Dad will expect, what he'll try next. If we don't know either, it'll be harder for him.'

'What about your clothes, your school stuff? Your furniture?' She seems to find it hard to believe that all of that will have to stay where it is.

I lean forward. 'Mum? Where did you see Dad? How did you know it was him?'

Mum has almost stopped crying, thank God, so she can talk properly. It doesn't sound like she's taken any pills either. Hopefully they're inside the apartment too. I know that's mean, but they'll make things worse.

'After I dropped you girls off, I went to buy some groceries and a little gift for Bobby, to say thank you. I parked down the end of our street where he lives, to drop it off to him and tell him how well the car was running. Bobby was on the phone, talking to his mother. He said she'd heard knocking, had gone out to see who was visiting. Thank God for nosy neighbours!'

'You mean Dad was at our front door?' The skin on my face pulls tight like a rubber band. I can't get my mouth closed.

'I thought maybe it was someone from my work. I prayed it was. But Bobby took me up on the roof of his building. You can see all up the street from there. Your father was just standing, leaning against his car, smoking a damn cigarette like it was the most natural thing in the world –' She takes a shaky breath. 'Most natural thing you could imagine, waiting for your wife so you could beat her up and drag her home again.'

'What did Bobby say?'

She laughs shortly. 'He wanted to go down and beat the crap out of him. I had to yell at him to make him see sense. Your father would just get him arrested and see that he was sent away for as long as possible.'

Her words settle inside me like slugs of lead. 'So he's here. We need to get moving. The sooner, the better.'

'I'll catch a bus home,' Dobie says quickly. 'Just drop me off on the other side of the park.' She hesitates. 'Is there any way I can go to your place sometime, pack up your stuff for you and send it somewhere? I want to help.'

'Not a good idea,' Mum says. 'It's too dangerous.'

I take stock of what I own – is there anything worth the risk? Dad will have used a private detective. He's got one who works for his law firm. Would he pay the guy to hang around for a week or two, just in case? Possibly, especially if we get away again. He'd be really mad this time.

'No, don't bother. We're better off leaving it all, aren't we, Mum?'

'Yes, you're right. Just as well I've been sending money to Lesley. It won't be so hard to start again.'

'Lesley is Mum's sister,' I tell Dobie. 'We went to her first when we left. Big mistake. Made us too easy to find.'

'Um...' Dobie's face has gone bright red.

'What? What's wrong?'

Mum whips around in her seat. 'Have you seen something? Is it his car?'

'No, it's …' Dobie swallows. 'It's Midnight. What about the kitten?'

CHAPTER 20
Dobie

I didn't want to say anything in case I set Goody's mum off again, but I had to.

They both stare at me like I've just said there's a dead body in their apartment. Well, there will be if they leave the kitten there with no food.

'It's OK,' I gabble, 'I'll go and feed it, or take it home, or find a home for it, or something…' They're still staring at me; no one's saying anything and I don't know whether to keep talking or shut up. I shut up.

Goody turned pale but now there are two red spots burning on her face and her chin juts out. 'I'm not leaving Midnight behind,' she says.

'We have to. We... I'm not going back there again. If he saw us...' Goody's mum is gasping, her hands gripping each other like she's drowning.

'You don't have to go back. I will. I'll take the key to Bobby, get him to fetch Midnight for me.'

'No! You can't! I don't want to involve anyone else.'

'Then I'll go myself, sneak up the stairs from the other side where the garbage cans are.' Goody's voice is hard; she folds her arms and glares at us both.

'Oh, Melissa, why are you being like this? You know we have to... I...' Her mouth starts trembling and I think she's going to cry. Oh shit. Now what? But she opens her door and half-falls out of the car. 'I have to think for a moment, I have to...' She staggers away from the car, towards a row of huge, marble-topped graves, and sits down on one of them, her face in her hands.

'You think I'm being stupid, or mean, don't you?' Goody stares out at her mother, her mouth twisting.

'Er, no, I...'

Although actually I do, just a little. If her dad is as violent as she says, it'll be a huge risk to go back for the kitten. Why won't she let me take care of it?

'Every time this happens, I lose my life. I lose my friends, all the things that are precious to me. I don't have anything of my own any more. No one to love me just for me.' Her voice wavers for a second, but she keeps going. 'I'm always the one who has to be tough, to look after her when she falls in a heap, like I'm the mum or something. If she'd just been stronger right from the start, made him stop beating her, stood up for herself... she's so useless sometimes!'

'It's not that simple, you know.' I don't want to argue with her but I have to say something. 'It's not one big, fast, battle and then it's won. It's the same stuff, day after day, like chipping away at a big rock. If they chip in the right places, eventually there's nothing left to hold you up.'

That's what my mother did with me. I tried so hard with the physio, I was so determined; and every day she did the pity and the *isn't it really too hard on you?* routine. Fact is, I gave in. I've spent all this time and energy hating her and getting back at her. I should have spent it getting fit again.

'It's easy for you to say.' Goody's almost spitting, she's so mad. 'You've got a family, a big house, lots of money. You can have anything you want.'

'I wanted to dance. I'd give up all the rest for that.'

'So what's stopping you? I want to be a nurse. Fat chance! I'm never in one school long enough to keep my grades up.'

I'm trying hard not to get angry with her. I can see that underneath she's really frightened, but I guess she has a right to be mad too.

She asked a question. What *is* stopping me? My injured shoulder, that's what. *Except they told me there was a chance I could dance again, if I kept up the physio and had two more operations.* Two more! In that hospital, with the zombie drugs and the pain and the possibility that it might not work. It was too hard. I couldn't do it... *then you didn't really want it badly enough!*

'You didn't tell me you wanted to be a nurse.' If I talk to Goody, I might calm her down and then we can make a move from here. I've got an idea. If her mum agrees.

'What's the point? It's never going to happen.' One big tear rolls down her face. She ignores it and jerks her head towards her mum. 'D'you want to go and get her? We can't stay here all day.'

'Goody, don't be mad with her. She can't help it. She's had all the brave part beaten out of her. You *are* tough and strong. That's the way it is. It won't be like this forever, you know.'

'I hope not.' She sniffs. 'I made her leave, you know, after he cut her with the knife. I was so scared all the time. I had this teddy bear that I dragged everywhere. I even stuffed him in my schoolbag when I went to school. I thought Teddy might save us – stupid, huh?' She shakes her head. 'But after he cut her, I knew no one would save us. Mum wouldn't go to the police. She said Dad had the cops in his pocket, that it was no use. So I made her leave. I said I'd run away on my own if she didn't come with me. So all this is really my fault.'

'No! Don't say that!' Suddenly a whole lot of things fall into place, like a jigsaw puzzle arranging itself on the table. 'Go get your mum. Quick. We'll go back to Middle Gate, park a couple of blocks away, and I'll fetch Midnight. Your dad doesn't know me.

The way I look, I'll just be another punk on the street, right?'

Goody's eyes light up. 'You'd do that for me? Truly?'

'Sure. It's the safest option. And in a couple of weeks, I can pack up your things and send them on to you.' I give her a hug. 'But I'm going to really miss you.'

'Me too.' She hugs me back. 'Another friend left behind.'

'Don't think like that. Things will work out, I have this feeling. For now, let's just worry about the kitten and you two getting away safely.'

'OK.' She leans out of the car window. 'Mum! Let's go!'

Her mum looks blankly at the car and then wanders over. I don't like the way she's acting. 'Is she going to be all right?'

'She will be, even if I have to shake her

into it,' Goody says grimly. 'Mum, get with it. We're taking Dobie back to our apartment. She's going to get Midnight for me.'

'But your father will see us.' She slowly slides in behind the wheel. 'We need to get out of town, not go back.'

'No, Mum, we'll park a couple of blocks away and Dad won't see us. Come on, the sooner we do it, the better.' She jiggles her mum's arm and finally the engine's rumbling and we're on our way.

My stomach's full of tiny, leaping frogs. I try to breathe evenly, in, out, in, out, and not think about what might go wrong. 'What does your dad look like? Apart from the car he's driving.'

'He's tall, with blond hair and a beard, but he's a bit fat too. Is he still fat, Mum?'

Goody's mum nods. 'Yes, even more than before. Probably eating out all the time. He played football at uni but…'

'Anyway, he's big. You can't miss him.' Goody bites a fingernail and rips it away down to the quick. She must have frogs inside too, I think.

We stop talking and sit close together in the back seat. I can hear her breathing like me, a bit too fast, as she attacks another nail. I rub my sweaty hands on my new jeans. All too soon we're in Middle Gate, pulling up under a scraggly tree.

'Here's my key,' Goody says, handing it to me. It's warm from being in her pocket. 'We're 402, remember? I'll come with you to the corner and show you the entrance to the back stairs.'

'You should stay here,' her mum says.

'Dobie won't know where to go. I have to at least take her to the corner,' Goody snaps. Her mum slides down in her seat and closes her eyes.

'Let's go,' I say, before I can change my mind. Now the frogs are leaping around in time to the huge drum in my heart.

We walk to the first corner and along the next street. A fat cloud crosses the sun and its dark shadow slides over the buildings. At the next corner, Goody stops and I bump into her.

'Sorry.'

'Why are you whispering?' she says, and tries to smile. 'That second building, the one with the blue windows on the second floor – that's ours. You have to go past the garbage cans and through the grey door where it says Fire Exit.'

'Won't it be locked?'

'Not around here. If there's anyone in the stairwell, just walk past them no matter what they're doing. Don't even say hello.'

I'm not going to ask what they might be doing. I've got imagination, that's enough. 'Do you want anything else apart from Midnight?'

She hesitates. 'My notebook, the one I write all my poems in. That's all.'

'OK.' I take a deep breath. 'Wish me luck.'

'You don't need luck. You just need to be careful.'

I walk away from her towards the grey door, my legs shaky. I pull the door open, head up the stairs, keep going fast even when I start to pant. The key is all ready to go in the lock, slide, turn, click. I'm inside. That was easy – I think. Where is the kitten? Where is Goody's notebook?

For one horrible moment I think the kitten has been taken, but then I spy it on her mum's bed, curled up asleep. The notebook is next to the futon. I pick up both of them and the kitten squawks. Where is the key? Did I leave it in the door? No, it's in my back pocket. Great. Let me out of here.

Midnight claws his way up my T-shirt and cuddles into my neck. I hold him in place, tuck the notebook under my arm and leave. Down the stairs, out the door, across the concrete, along to the corner. The street is deadly quiet. I can't quite believe it. I search around, walk up and down. It doesn't change a thing.

Goody has disappeared.

CHAPTER 21
Melissa

I watch Dobie walk across to our building and shiver. God, I hope she's OK. Now I know what Mum means when she insists that we never involve anyone else. It's too scary. Bad enough for us, but when I think of what could happen to Dobie...

She disappears inside and I relax a little. It should only take her a few minutes, then she'll be back and we can hit the road. If Dad is where Mum said he was, he'll be around the other side of our building, watching the entrance. Does he plan to stay there all day? I'd better keep out of sight in case he decides to cruise around the block.

Behind me across the street is a low brick wall and a few scrubby bushes. If I crouch down, the wall will almost hide me. As I cross the street, a car pulls up beside me. I nearly have a heart attack, but it's not a Mercedes. It's a low, blue, sporty thing. The driver's window is open but I only see who it is at the last moment, then it's too late to do anything except stand there like a dummy.

'Hello, Melissa. Why don't you get in?' It's Dad's private detective, Louie or Lonny or something, smirking at me like he's been so clever, finding me. He must've been watching the other side of the building while Dad took the front. 'Come on, be sensible. We've already got your mum.'

'No!' I shout. That acts like a starter's gun and I take off, running full tilt down the street, back to where Mum parked the car, looking for Dad's car, praying I'll get there in time. Too bad if Louie chases me, too bad about Dobie, I can't go back and tell her, I have to get to Mum. There, our car is still where she parked it, is she still inside?

Where's Dad? Oh God, he's standing next to it. She's still sitting in the driver's seat. She hasn't got out. Stay there, Mum, stay there!

I rush up to the car, lean against it, gasping for air. 'Go away! Go away!' I try to shout but my voice comes out all strangled.

'Melissa. You've grown. You look lovely.'

What is this? He's smiling, big white teeth, pretending it's a happy reunion, happy family, what a lie, what a lie! 'Get away from her.'

'No, I can't do that. You and your mother are coming home with me. This silliness has gone on long enough.'

Louie pulls up in his car, but Dad signals him and he doesn't get out.

'We're not going with you. Leave us alone.' I sound like a whiny five-year-old, but I'm not giving up. 'Mum, you stay where you are.' Mum says nothing but I can see her shaking

from where I am standing. She won't be able
to stop him if he tries to drag her to his car.
What can I do? What can I do?

'If you don't go away, I'll call the cops.'
I know that won't work but I have to say
something.

'I doubt that the police around here
bother with little family tiffs,' he says.
'They'd only come out for murders.'

He's so damn sure of himself, so calm.
He knows he's got the power to do anything
he wants and no one will stop him. Well,
this time he's got it all wrong.

I walk around the car and move up close
to him. I have to look up to face him squarely
but I do it, planting my feet solidly on the
ground, bracing myself.

'You don't understand. We are not coming
with you. We are staying here. We are never
going to live with you, or anywhere near
you, ever again.' It's like a litany, a chant, a
song that rolls out of me. 'We hate you. We

wouldn't live with you if you were the last person on earth. Go away, you rotten, mean, horrible man.'

His eyes flicker and for one moment, I think I've won, that my words have actually had some impact. Then he says, 'You will both do exactly as I say. Or you will be sorry. *Very* sorry.'

'Didn't you hear what she said? She told you to piss off.'

It's Dobie! She won't be able to help, no one can help us now, but it's so good to hear her voice!

'Go away, whoever you are. This is none of your business,' Dad snaps.

'It is my business. These are my friends and they don't want you around.'

'If you interfere, you will be sorry too, I can guarantee that.' Dad's voice has turned low and nasty, and that old crawling spider feeling runs up my neck.

Dobie walks around to where we're standing and hands Midnight and my notebook to Mum. 'What are you going to do?' she says. 'Beat up all of us at once?'

'I told you, kid. Mind your own business. Take your smelly cat and get lost.' He tries to reach into the car and grab Midnight. I knock his hand aside and he bangs it on the window frame.

'Don't you touch him! He's *my* cat.'

'Don't you tell me what to do, miss,' he snarls. He checks his hand for injury. 'You need to learn some manners. Now, get your mother out of that car and let's go.'

He grabs me by the arm and pulls me around, trying to open Mum's door at the same time. I stagger sideways and hit my elbow on the car. Pain shoots up my arm, but even faster the red haze that I've tried so hard to control roars up in front of my eyes. I let it take over, and launch myself, screaming, at my father, punching and pounding with my fists, aiming mostly for his face.

'You little –' At first he tries to defend himself and push me off, but I'm too strong, I'm too angry, I'm going to kill him if I just get half a chance. I leap up with fingers gouging, going for his eyes. Suddenly I'm on the ground, winded, my head ringing. What happened, did he hit me?

I hear this yell and look up. It's Dobie. She's pushing him backwards, away from the car. No, don't, Dobie. God, look at his face, no, he's going to hurt you. Stop!

But it's too late, he backhands her, sends her flying into the side of the car. She makes one funny crying sound and crumples down. Has he killed her? No, she's still crying, at least I can hear that.

And I can hear something else too, someone else, talking. I try to get up and the world sways a bit. I feel sick, but I have to get up, I have to do something, I have to get Mum. I manage to stand up even though my head's pounding. Who is that? Someone else is standing by the front of our car. Louie? No, it's Bobby, with a mobile phone. He was the one who was talking, into the phone. Now he's talking again, to us, to Dad. I blink hard, try to focus.

'The cops are on their way. Next street, in fact. So don't try to make a run for it.'

Just as he says that, a cop car pulls up, lights flashing, and two cops jump out. Bobby seems to know them. He talks and points, Dad looks sick. Louie is nowhere in sight.

I bend down to Dobie. She's hunched over her arm, her bad arm, whimpering. It's the worst sound in the world. She tries to say something but I can't hear her. I touch her shoulder but she shakes me off. She lifts her head, stares past me to the two cops.

'You have to arrest him for assault,' she says. Her voice is so clear and strong, tears well up in my eyes. 'I'm pressing charges. Call my father.'

'She... she fell,' my father says. 'It was an accident.'

I straighten up. 'No, it wasn't. You hit her, straight after you hit me. I'm pressing charges too.'

Now the tears are running down my face but I don't care. They're not weak tears, they're tears of victory.

CHAPTER 22
Dobie

When the painkillers finally kick in, I lie back in the hospital bed and stare at the ceiling. White tiles, fourteen along by twenty two across, that's –

'Hello, sweetheart.'

I turn my head too fast and pain stabs through my shoulder and neck. It's Dad. 'Hi.' What's he doing here? That's right, I told them to call him.

'The doctor said you're OK, no major muscle or bone damage.' He tries a smile but it looks more like a grimace. 'How on earth did you get involved with those people?'

'Hey, *those people* are my friends!' I glare at him. He'd better not have come here to lecture me.

'You could've been killed, or badly hurt, Deborah,' he says. 'I don't take that lightly.'

'Dad, since when have you really cared about what happens to me?' His face pales but I'm not letting him off the hook. 'It's a bit late now to be going on about *those people*. It's the one at home that's my problem. Where is my darling mother?'

Instead of going off at me for being rude about Mother dear, he rubs his ear and looks away. 'She's... not coming.'

'How predictable.' And just like that, I dismiss her from my brain. I no longer want to waste any time or energy on her. Delete.

'Now about your friend and her father,' Dad says, changing the subject.

'Where is she? More to the point, where is *he*?'

'He's in custody. He's been formally charged and the bail hearing is tomorrow morning.'

'He won't get bail, will he?' God, Goody and her mum would be right back where they started.

'Not if they give the police full statements. Your friend already has, but her mother was too upset.'

'What about me? I want to make a statement too.'

'Well, I tried to get you out of that – '

'I don't want you to get me out of it. I want to help.' Doesn't he understand anything? 'Will they refuse him bail if we all stand up and say how obsessed he is?'

'Possibly. It depends on his lawyer, how well he defends him.' Dad fidgets in his chair. 'I don't think you understand the ramifications of all this.'

What? That some guy has been terrorising his wife and daughter for years, and no one has had the guts to stop him?

'Fill me in, Dad.' I try not to be too sarcastic but it still leaks out, and his mouth tightens.

'If he's convicted of assault, he'll be disbarred as a lawyer. He might not go to jail, though, he might be given a community order instead.'

'But that means he'd be out and harassing them again!'

'That's why a lot of women don't testify. And when they do...'

I think about it and go cold. 'There was something in the paper about a guy who shot his ex-wife. That's what you're talking about, aren't you?'

'Yes, and I don't want you in the middle of it.'

'So, just leave them to it, you reckon. Too bad if they get hurt or killed.'

'That's not what I mean at all.' He jumps up, his face angry. 'There are things like restraining orders, and if he offended again, he would be given a sentence.'

'Great choice, huh? Testify against the guy and risk him tracking you down, or run again and let him off, and he'll still track you down. Shit.'

'That's life, Deborah.'

Great, Dad. Wonderful philosophy you've got there.

'He's right.' Goody's voice is like music to me.

'Hey, you're OK!' I say, grinning at her like a loony. Then I realise the door's been open the whole time. How much has she heard?

'Yeah, I am,' she says, ducking her head a little. 'And your dad is right. My father could still hurt both of us. But I'm sick of running. The fear is the same either way, but if we stay here, we can get some kind of protection.'

'But will your mum testify?' Or more likely, would she end up in a psych ward?

'I think she might.' She turns her face towards me and I gasp. She has a huge black eye and three little stitches on her cheekbone. 'When he hit me, I think that was the turning point for her.'

I glance at Dad, and the horror on his face is almost laughable. He says, 'If you and your mother are staying here, maybe I can help her out with a job.'

'That'd be great, Dad,' I say. Maybe there's hope for him yet.

'But you, young lady,' he says, turning to me, 'are not staying at Village Gate.'

'I am not going back to Barton, even if you tie me to their fancy front gate.'

Boarding school is starting to look like a real possibility. I swallow hard.

'I don't want to stay at Village Gate either,' Goody says suddenly. 'It's the pits.'

Dad gazes at both of us and nods. 'Let's look for a compromise – a school we might all be happy with.'

'Everyone except Mother, you mean.' I don't think he realises what a battle he'll have.

'I'll deal with that later.' He gives Goody his business card and says her mum should call him as soon as she's ready.

'Thanks,' Goody says, and stares at it like it's going to bite her.

After he's gone, I ask her, 'What are you really going to do?'

'Testify against the bastard, and make sure Mum does too.' She puts the business card in her pocket. 'After that, try to start living a half-normal life, I guess. It feels weird. And scary. But not as scary as running. And we'll get to see Aunty Lesley again.'

'Is your mum going to file for divorce too?'

Her mouth twists. 'I wish. She said she's scared it will make him worse, but how can he get worse than he is already? I don't know...'

'Hey, you've got me, you know. Maybe we could both learn kung fu or something.'

She laughs. 'Yeah, right. You wouldn't be able to, would you?' Too late, she slaps her hand over her mouth. 'Sorry, I shouldn't have said that.'

'It's OK.' I fiddle with the bed cover, pick a thread and pull it out. 'I've... decided to have the extra operations and go back to physio.'

Her eyes widen. 'Really? What will that mean? You can dance again? That would be so cool. You're so brilliant at it.'

'Slow down!' I love the way she's so happy for me, even if I haven't done anything yet. 'It's going to be a long hard road. I might not make it.'

'But you're going to give it a go,' she says. 'You're going to fight the dragons.'

'Yeah, well, so are you.'

She hoists herself up on the bed next to me, on my good side, and pulls two bars of chocolate out of her bag. 'I got them out of the machine. Want one?'

I think about what I'm going to look like in a leotard, how much harder it is to glide and leap and spin with ten extra kilos hanging off me. 'No, thanks. You need chocolate more than me.'

She shoves the bars back in her bag. 'I'll save it for later. Now what school do you think we should go to?'

Breaking Dawn
DONNA SHELTON
Is friendship forever? Secrets, betrayal, remorse and suicide.

Don't Even Think It
HELEN ORME
One family's terrible secret.

Gun Dog
PETER LANCETT
Does having a gun make you someone? Does it make you strong or does it actually make you weak? Stevie is about to find out.

Marty's Diary
FRANCES CROSS
How to handle step-parents.

Seeing Red
PETER LANCETT
The pain and the pleasure of self-harm.

See You on the Backlot
THOMAS NEALEIGH
Tony is 'Clown Prince of the Sideshow'. He has carnival in his blood, but the fun and laughter stops backstage.

Stained
JOANNE HICHENS
Crystal is a teenage mum in despair. Can't anyone see the tragedy unfolding? Her only hope is Grace next door.

The Finer Points of Becoming Machine
EMILY ANDREWS
Emma is a mess, like her suicide attempt, but everyone wants her to get better, don't they?

The Only Brother
CAIAS WARD
Sibling rivalry doesn't end at the grave – Andrew is still angry with his only brother, so angry he's hitting out at everyone, including his dad.

The Questions Within
TERESA SCHAEFFER
Scared to be gay?

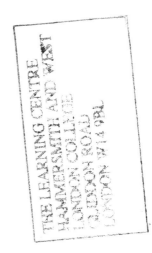